I0574970

A PLACE TO STAND

BECCA LYNN MATHIS

A Place to Stand

Copyright © 2020 by Becca Lynn Mathis

This is a work of fiction. Names, characters, places, and incidents either are the product of the author's imagination or are used fictitiously. Any resemblance to actual persons, living or dead, events, or locales is entirely coincidental.

All rights reserved. No part of this book may be reproduced in any form, including by an electronic or mechanical means, including information storage and retrieval systems, without permission in writing from the publisher, except by a reviewer who may quote brief passages in a review.

First paperback edition November 2020

ISBN 978-1-7331626-5-4 (hardcover)

ISBN 978-1-7331626-4-7 (paperback)

ISBN 978-1-7331626-3-0 (ebook)

EDITOR— Natasha Raulerson (www.natasharaulerson.com)

COVER DESIGN—Joolz & Jarling – Julie Nicholls & Uwe Jarling

INTERIOR FORMATTING & DESIGN—T.E. Black Designs; www.teblackdesigns.com

www.beccalynnmathis.com

This book would never have happened if not for my absolutely wonderful husband, my resident dragon, Kevin. Your encouragement has been absolutely priceless through this entire process. Thank you for always being the most amazing brainstormer an author could ever ask for and for having the sort of patience that lets you love me even when I spend endless nights at my computer instead of snuggled against you. I love you. This one is DEFINITELY for you!

To all of my beta readers and my editor: Natasha, Ben, Stina, Richie, Ace, Melanie, Andie, and Myri. You folks really helped this story to shine and I freaking love you for it!

To my Twitter fam, for putting up with all my ramblings and hair pulling rants as I tried to wrangle this sucker into submission.

To my sister-from-another-mister, Trishinator, for always encouraging me and for being an inspiration with your crazy ridiculous work ethic.
And to the rest of my friends in the Texas group chat, for being there at all weird hours of the day with a funny meme or other sanity-saving measures.

To all my packmates near and far.
Particularly those who loved Lynn's story as much as I did.

And, most importantly, to my family, who put up with my short-tempered days, my sleepy days, my absent days, and my days where I just went through the motions because my mind was still in these pages. You mean the world to me. I love you.

PROLOGUE

ZACCHAEUS
Undisclosed Location, November 2019

I CLICKED play on the laptop, which started the video stream through my conference call with the other two oldest vampires in the world. On my screen—and presumably on theirs—a white werewolf and a grey one ran through the woods, their breaths coming out in little puffs of fog. As the tear gas canisters from the vampires of my coterie hit the ground in the video, I watched the faces of the other two elders in anticipation. The delay was hell thanks to the multiple layers of security bouncing our signals all across the globe, but it was necessary to keep our locations secret from one another. Elsewise, we'd be putting ourselves in danger of assassination.

Kitashihime's arms were folded into the opposite sleeves of her kimono, her posture as rigid and unyielding as she was. Her black hair was pulled into a smooth bun held in place with hair sticks, though her perfectly manicured bangs brushed her forehead and framed her face. Her shrewd almond-shaped dark eyes watched her screen, her lips pressed into an impassive line.

Vsevolod, on the other hand, sat almost lazily in his leather wingback chair, his relaxed expression belying the violence he was more than capable of. His sharp, icy blue eyes had crow's feet in the corners. He wore a black turtleneck under his brown leather coat, his grey-black beard brushing the sherpa-lined collar. The beard softened his severely squared jawline, and his hair was cropped short this time. Last I had seen him, his hair had been longer, pulled into a tail that ran down his back.

Neither seemed particularly interested in the video.

And then, they blinked shortly after the first vampire dusted. Damn delay. I was almost surprised they reacted at all. Kitashihime was a few centuries younger than myself—too young to remember the last *purgatum*. But Vsevolod was at least a century older than me. He watched the carnage back then as our already small numbers nearly died out altogether, coterie by coterie.

The yelps and snarls and scrabbling of the vampire-versus-werewolf fight in the video continued. I clicked pause just after the white wolf sank her teeth into the thigh of the last vampire. He had been mid-swing, and his axe buried itself in the nearest tree as he turned to ash.

I switched to the camera on my laptop. "Only one vampire walked away from this fight," I told them. "A coward who ran early on. As you can see, this she-wolf is quite formidable." I pulled up the paused video. "Her ability is… problematic."

"True," Vsevolod said, rolling the 'R' ever so slightly. "But she is one girl. Wolf she may be, but young she is, easy problem."

His English was never particularly great.

I let them drink in the sight of her a moment longer before switching to the camera again. "The pack here did us a favor when they had her kill Frederick. He was quite the thorn in our side. Though I must admit that for a vampire who used to be a werewolf, his research provided a great distraction, at least locally."

I crossed my hands behind my back.

Vsevolod and Kitashihime's eyes narrowed, almost in sync.

"He was a wolf first?" Kitashihime's clipped voice was dark and gravel-torn—an old voice in the face of a woman who could easily pass for thirty. I had nearly forgotten her voice was so deep.

"How is possible?"

Poor Vsevolod. His English would likely improve if he could simply be bothered to surround himself with more diverse company.

I smiled—bared my teeth at them, really. "Oh, didn't you know? Frederick DuBois kept meticulously detailed records of his experiments. He dropped his files directly to me, of course, but what he used to be is the entire reason he was performing his experiments in the first place."

I studied the two of them for a moment before continuing. Their careful masks of neutrality were now back in place.

"Anyway, we will need to keep these local wolves occupied, too busy to send their she-wolf our way." I spread my hands. "In fact, we'll have to assume that as of now, all the North American packs know of this she-wolf's ability, and the rest of the world's packs will know in short order—as will the church, who will scramble to get their hands on her. And since we must make such an assumption, it is time to force the werewolves out of hiding."

"Distract the wolves." Vsevolod leaned back lazily, waving a hand. "Capture her."

"Make her our weapon," Kitashihime added.

I cracked my neck and pulled my lips even further from my teeth. "I am so glad you could anticipate such a decision. Of course I will bring her into my coterie, and I'll wipe out her pack when I do."

"Good." Vsevolod's video feed went black.

"Be careful not to kill her," Kitashihime warned. "The wolves grow far too confident in your territory. You will need her to crush them."

I nodded once. "Of course."

Her feed went black, and I closed the program. A handful of keystrokes later, the hard drive in the laptop was reformatting, erasing the video and any connection I had made with the other two elders.

As I left my office, my assistant Ally, a young vampire who was positively eager to rise through the ranks, stood to greet me.

I handed the laptop to her. "Take this to Denver and pawn it. Have a new one on my desk tomorrow."

"Sure." She tossed her sleek brown hair over her shoulder and batted her eyelashes over her big brown eyes. "Everyone's out for dinner, Zee. Wanna make use of that conference table?"

She shrugged her cardigan off her shoulders. She wore only a black bra underneath. And it perfectly matched her black pencil skirt. As she bent to place the laptop in her bag, I couldn't help but notice the tantalizingly delicious things her sky high heels did for her ass.

Oh yes, she was a *very* good assistant.

I smiled at her as I loosened my tie. It was almost a shame she'd never make it to a hundred.

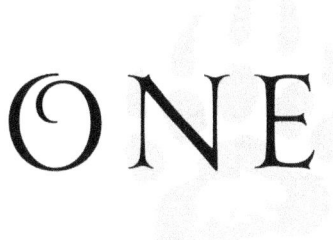

ONE

KRISTOS
New Orleans, November 2019

THERE WASN'T anything special about the sports bar, it barely had good beer. But it had people. Not enough to be crowded on a weeknight, but enough that I was just another guy drinking alone at the bar.

Oh yea. And the cute little bartender was savvy enough to recognize when a customer wasn't interested in chatting.

I took another long sip of my beer as I considered the voicemail the Colorado Springs alpha had left me.

"I got a werewolf here that can dust a vamp with her bite. I figure you might know something."

He wasn't wrong.

She was a *purgatum*, and the first in centuries to boot.

Fuck.

I drained my glass and dialed Sheppard's number. When he answered, he put me on speakerphone and filled me in on what he had seen of her capabilities. I didn't need the narration. I knew from the voicemail alone what he had taken into his pack.

Sixteen hundred years ago, I would have begged her to take the bear from me, even if it killed me.

"Her jaws sunk into his neck as she clawed into his chest, and it was like time caught up with him," Sheppard said. "He turned to a desiccated corpse and then to dust, right there in his cave."

Twelve hundred years ago, I would have handed her ass directly to the vampires and walked away.

"She turned that crazed wolf back to human," Sheppard said.

Five hundred years ago, I wouldn't have even returned the call—not that there were even phones then. She wasn't in danger. She had a pack.

"And I just killed three more with just a bite," she said. The *consanguinea*. No, the *purgatum*.

It was a single line, a matter-of-fact statement about her recent vampire kills. But I heard the fear in her voice anyway. And it pulled at a bone-deep instinct I had thought long gone. An instinct I thought died in an abandoned manor in Bulgaria twelve hundred years ago.

She needed protection.

So, I told Sheppard about the only other *consanguinea* I had ever heard of like her—the one the church had culled because it was a threat to their mission to save humanity. Hell, the church even had to get their hands dirty since they couldn't get any of us bears to do it. We literally could not.

When I hung up the phone, I paid my bar tab and went back to the motel next door to pack my things. I took my room key to the front office, where I found a frazzled couple dragging their uncooperative toddler toward the front desk. I caught the eye of the dad—who looked more like a pack mule with all the bags he carried—and pointedly placed my room key on the counter.

"It's paid for the next couple of nights," I told him before looking at the front desk clerk. She was barely more than a kid herself, with dark hair and big brown eyes. I read her name tag. "Hey Monica, I'm checking out of 214. Transfer the rest of my nights to this lovely family, alright? Take good care of them."

"That's really not necessary," the woman sputtered. She had blonde hair that probably started the day in a sleek ponytail, but it now hung in a limp mess from the back of her head like her hair tie had simply given up on life. She managed to get the uncooperative toddler quiet by handing him her phone, which started blaring some obnoxious child's song about a shark.

I waved off her protest and gestured to the bag I had slung over my shoulder and the tackle box that held my jeweler's tools. "Obviously, I'm not gonna use it. And I'm not concerned with the refund, since it takes so long to process through the bank."

"We sure appreciate it," the pack mule of a father told me. His certain tone left no room for argument, and his wife gave me a weary smile.

Monica gave me a receipt for the room nights used and had me sign for the new rooms as the kid's shark song started playing over again. The little one bounced on one of the couches in the lobby as he watched the screen, and the mom tried to wrangle the phone from him.

I headed out to my truck, a blue two-door Ford F150. She was always a bit dirty—until it rained, at least—and she had any number of minor scratches and bumps from all the miles I'd put on her already. But she was reliable as hell and easy to repair. And she was the only lady I'd had any kind of lasting relationship with in recent memory.

It wasn't until I was five miles down the road that I even knew what I was doing.

Fuck.

I was heading to Colorado Springs.

Fuck.

I wasn't even sure how long it would take me to get there from New Orleans. So I checked it on my phone. Twenty-two-and-a-half hours. And that was assuming I didn't make any stops.

FUCK!

I stopped myself from smacking the heel of my hand into the steering wheel, an action that would have necessitated costly repairs, and instead balled my hand into a fist so hard my knuckles cracked.

This stupid instinct to protect *consanguinea* had been quiet for goddamn *centuries*, but now is when it crops up? Ludicrous. This was a bad idea. Clearly an unignorable bad idea, but a bad idea nonetheless. The last time I tried to protect a *consanguinea*, it went very, very poorly for everyone involved.

I checked the map on my phone and shook my head again at the time estimate. Twenty-two-and-a-half hours.

As much as I wanted to ignore the *purgatum* even existed, I couldn't. My actions ceased being my own because I knew better. Protecting her—and those like her—was exactly what I was created to do.

And if I could protect her from the church, who was likely to cull her too, then maybe I could correct the wrongdoings of my past as well.

TWO

A PRIEST once told me that everything in your life is inexorably linked to everything else in your life, no matter how long it's been or how far away from it you are.

I wanted him to be wrong.

By the time I'd found myself in the New World, my life had already been far too long. All the same, I found myself in a public house somewhere in the then-colony of Virginia, which was known for its verdant fields of tobacco. I had traveled to meet a jeweler there, to discuss some new technique he claimed to have discovered for setting stones flush with the metal. Problem was, when he finally arrived to explain what he'd found, it became clear he'd simply rediscovered methods the Romans had used centuries ago.

History truly does have a way of repeating itself.

As he left, I asked for another beer from the tender.

Beer has come a long way since colonial times. For starters, it tastes better. The alcohol content was lower back then, though that meant nothing to me anyway. My metabolism made sure of that. But it tasted a hell of a lot better than the dirt water from the well and was probably safer to drink anyway, at least for the humans.

Better than that, these days, you can go to practically any convenience or grocery store and purchase bottles of it. But back then? If you weren't making it yourself, you had to stop in at a tavern. Even then, you were drinking beer poured from a barrel into a mug made of either glass or tin or wood. This particular establishment used heavy glass mugs, which let the taste of the brew shine.

I had my second mug down and had started my third when the werewolves arrived. There were five of them. I didn't know their names then, but I'll never forget them now. Abner. Matt. Sampson. Tobias. John. A small pack by today's standards, but perfectly normal back then.

Anyhow, I smelled them when they came in— wildflower, spicy musk, earthy tobacco, warmth, and salty sea air all comingling with a wild undercurrent that told me clear as day there was about to be trouble. They seemed pleased, perhaps even prideful, and moved with the smooth grace of predators as they approached the counter.

"I can't believe you got five of them yourself before we even got in to back you up," the one with close cropped brown hair said excitedly to the shaggy blonde as the burly one ordered drinks for the pack.

The shaggy blonde clapped him on the shoulder, beaming as he did. "You got a couple on your own, too."

"I know," he said. "But it'll be a long while before I can match you." There was no mistaking the admiration in his voice.

If they were talking about vampires—and I suspected they were—he must have been newly turned, relatively-speaking.

It took barely a moment beyond their entrance

for them to smell me. I was the only other patron left in the public house.

The shaggy blond eyed me, his musky scent sharpening and his lip curling as he sized me up. Werewolves never know what to make of me, and—if his scent was anything to go by—this one was no exception.

I took a long sip of my beer and tried not to sigh at them as I leaned back in my chair.

"You'll get there," the shaggy blond said over his shoulder as he put his back against the bar.

The bartender poured a mug of beer for everyone, and waited expectantly as the burly one pulled coins from his pocket and placed them on the counter. The tender had neither told them the cost nor asked for more coin beyond what was provided.

They'd been here before. Likely, I was in their territory. Maybe the jeweler had been a setup? Had the church found me again? Hmm. Not likely. The jeweler hadn't been lying about his discovery. It just wasn't actually a novel innovation.

The new wolf and the shaggy blond grabbed their mugs almost absentmindedly as they pushed off the bar. The new wolf was full of swagger, puffing out his chest as he took deliberate steps toward my table. The shaggy blond paced like a seasoned hunter.

Dammit.

I took another sip from my mug to hide my scowl as the shaggy blonde pulled a chair over and sat close enough to me that I could feel the warmth of his body against my leg. His dark-haired friend sat on the other side of me, nearly as close, as the burly one leaned against the counter and made small talk with the tender and his other two pack mates.

The blond one took a deep drink from his mug and then made a show of sniffing at me, his nostrils flaring as he set his square jaw. "Well, well, well, what have we here?"

"Something better left alone." I held his gaze. "The important thing is I know what you and your friends are, and I know you don't want this fight."

The new wolf looked at the shaggy blond, eagerness in his expression. He was smaller than his friend, but he seemed scrappy. He glanced between the blond and me. Something passed between the two of them, and the new wolf dropped his chin as the corner of his mouth pulled into a vicious smirk. "The only things that don't smell human are others of us, and vampires."

I gestured to my mug and made a show of finishing the beer in it. "The latter of which I, clearly, am not."

The pale blond snorted in derision. "You don't smell like one of us, so you must be."

Only there was a question in his tone. I was pretty sure he was poking at me to get him to tell him what I really was.

The new wolf lunged across the table at me. "I'll take you down myself, you bloodsucker!"

No surprise that one made the first move.

No surprise he jumped to conclusions either.

The shaggy blond's eyes widened in surprise as I backfisted the new wolf away from me, bloodying his nose as he flew into the nearby wall.

The shaggy blond smashed his half-empty mug on the table, leaving a jagged handle in his grip as broken glass and spilled beer dripped from the edge of the table. "Whatever the hell you are, you don't get to disrespect pack like that!"

The wolves at the counter stilled at the commotion. As did the tender. The blond's heart pounded in his chest as a low, almost inaudible growl started deep in his throat.

"You won't like what you find at the other end of this fight, pup," I said. "Drop it and walk away."

"The hell I will!" The pale blond threw a punch toward my face with that broken beer mug.

In a single motion, I dodged the fist and broke his wrist to get him to release his grip. I grabbed the broken handle myself and slammed it twice into his left eye as I stood. What was left of the handle shattered into the soft flesh of his eye socket, and I left it there as I pulled my fist away the second time. His howl of pain became decidedly animalistic as he clawed at the broken glass in his face.

It was the sound of a wolf about to change.

The burly one at the counter rushed to his side, ushering him out the door so the tender wouldn't see the transformation of his packmate. Humans simply couldn't handle the knowledge that certain folklore held an uncanny amount of accuracy.

Fuck these wolves.

And fuck this place.

I headed for the coat rack, but the new wolf swaggered into my path, his nose no longer bleeding, as the other two from the bar stepped between us and the door.

"Where do you think you're going?" The new wolf stepped closer to me. "We aren't done here."

I sighed and looked at each of the three wolves before me. "You don't want this fight either."

None of them would hold my gaze, but their bodies were tensed for the fight, their scents sharp.

"You start this," I said. "And I'll end it."

I considered the new wolf for a moment and pointed at him with two fingers. "You'll throw the first punch now that your friend's gone. When it misses," I gestured to the one who smelled like the sea, "your friend here is gonna step around behind me to try to get me to the ground. But he'll fail, and end up with broken ribs at best."

I shook my head and jerked my thumbs at the other two as I held the gaze of the new wolf. "But then you'll get the two of them to try to hold me so you can have an easy target. Now, your packmates here are taller than me, but they're not nearly as solid. They won't get a good grip, and it'll only take a hit or two from me before I've got you all revealing your true nature to the nice gentleman behind the counter there." I indicated the tender with a nod of my head in his direction.

"Just who the bloody hell do you think you are, stranger?" The new wolf puffed his chest. "We just took down our third brood!"

"Abner!" The one who smelled of earthy tobacco elbowed the new wolf. He eyed me and the tender meaningfully.

The tender's stern voice carried through the room as he pointed toward the door. "That's enough from you folks. Get out."

"You pups have only seen the vamps from this side of the Atlantic," I replied quietly. "The true heavy hitters aren't yet willing to risk travel to such a wild land."

No one moved.

The tender pulled a musket from under the counter and pointed it in our direction. "I'm not keen to repeat myself when I've been quite clear." He ratcheted back the hammer of the flintlock.

If only that poor man understood his gun could never actually threaten any of us.

Even so, the three wolves in front of me parted like the Red Sea to let me pass, but they circled around behind me and followed as I stepped into the grey dusk of almost-night.

I walked around the building toward the back of

the public house where the stables were, and ignored the wolves at my back. They weren't actually a threat, and I just wanted to get on my horse and be on my way.

But the new wolf—Abner—stepped into my path and cracked the knuckles of his fists.

I shook my head at him. "We're on the same side here."

He sucked on his teeth and tsked at me. "No, I don't think we are."

"You pups think you're top dogs with your latest kill," I said, keeping my voice a low rumble as I listened for where his friends were behind me. "But you aren't old enough to know what a vampire really is. Like I said, none of the truly powerful ones have migrated here yet, and none that were already here would let themselves be found by such a green and cocksure pack."

"I'll show you who's cocksure," Abner said, rolling his shoulder back for a punch as he stepped toward me.

I interrupted his motion with a backhanded fist to his gut, batting him out of my way and throwing him against one of the trees that formed an orderly line along the north side of the public house.

As he stood, he tore his shirt from his shoulders, letting the change take him to the ground again. He released a furious growl as his pants tore to shreds.

His friends behind me started to change as well.

God damn it all to hell.

As Abner rose on four grey and brown paws, the burly man emerged from the shadows behind the church next door. At his side was a large werewolf in brown and black. I didn't need the breeze to know that it was Abner's cocky friend from the bar—the shards of glass had mostly come out of his eye socket when he changed, but the cuts were deep and oozed dark blood around the remaining shards. He'd likely heal it just fine once he got all the glass out, but it surely made his change that much more uncomfortable.

I met the wolf's eyes as his hackles rose along his spine. The two wolves behind me slammed into my shoulders, but I grabbed each by their scruffs and pulled them over my head to toss them to the ground in front and away from me.

The burly man rushed me, wrapping his arms around my waist and taking me to the ground, which surprised me. I recovered and rolled over on top of him to slam my fist into his skull, but he kicked his knees up and managed to push me away from him with his feet. He then rolled back and kipped up before tearing his clothes off to change.

A change that happened in a blink.

He was the alpha.

He leapt at me, and the whole pack followed suit, landing on my shoulders and chest, biting to hold on and scrabbling at me with their claws. I pulled them from me one by one, throwing the one with glass in his face away from me and bashing my fist into the head of the black wolf that smelled of the sea. Bones crunched under my knuckles, but each of them shook off the injury and the pain, healing the damage as they jumped back into place.

I didn't want to have to fight a pack into submission, and I kept trying to hurt instead of kill, but they wouldn't stop coming at me. And their alpha was strong. His power kept them coming at me long after I'd have expected them to cut their losses.

And then the alpha sank his jaws into the meat where my neck met my shoulder.

White-hot rage tore through me.

The anger of a thousand misunderstood intentions and hundreds of unnecessary fights.

The bear had had enough of this pack's bullshit.

I batted the alpha away, his jaws taking a solid chunk out of the side of my neck, and kicked out of my boots. The injury healed as I changed, though my clothes tore to shreds.

Silence rang in my ears.

The wolves all took pause at my bear form, ears perked as I shook the scraps of fabric from me. I was barely a foot or so taller than them, but I was easily twice their size in muscle mass.

Then, almost as one, all of their ears pinned back and silent snarls crept across their faces.

The brown and black wolf launched himself at me again, and I lashed out with a claw at his face. The blow landed squarely into his half-healed eye socket. There was still glass in that wound—glass that only crunched deeper as I caved in half his face and dragged my claw down his neck.

So much for his eye healing just fine. That glass wasn't coming out without a fight.

The grey and brown wolf, Abner, lunged at me, but I caught the motion with my claw. I slammed him to the ground with a meaty crunch that I immediately recognized as his chest caving in and his spine crushing under the weight of my paw.

I had killed him.

Dammit!

I roared my fury at the pack and ran into the trees. The pack didn't follow me.

THREE

I T HAD BEEN TOO long since I'd let the bear run. In all my years, I had never once killed a wolf that wasn't crazed. I'd gotten close, seriously injured wolves who couldn't leave well enough alone. But I had never killed a stable wolf.

It took me hours to run off the rage and guilt. Hours to run from the sound of his last gasping breath. Hours to run from the feel of his spine crumbling under my paw. Hours of running through woods and tobacco fields and horse pastures, only to find myself right back at the spot where he'd died. The patch of dirt where I'd killed him.

I hadn't meant to kill any of them. Certainly not one so young. There was a lot of good that pup could have done. That wolf—Abner—had a very long life ahead of him. And I had truncated it.

It was full dark by then. The fatigue of the fight pulled at me, but I couldn't let myself sleep yet. The moon was barely a sliver that night, and the lights were out in the public house. But even in the dark, the starlight glinted off the wet patch of dirt where Abner fell. The air smelled more of wet earth than blood. The wolves must have tried to water down the bloodstain.

I had to make reparations. The pack didn't deserve to suffer because of me. But suffered, they did. And suffer they would still for the missing pack member. No money in this world could make up for that, but maybe I could. I had to.

I pushed the thought of sleep out of my head and snuck back to my horse, where I put some proper clothes on and tracked them, leading the sleepy beast along with me.

They had carried their fallen packmate past the post office on the south side of town. Hidden behind the building, I found their clothing stockpile—a wooden barrel with a false bottom containing several sets of clothes wrapped in a linen sheet—which told me they usually came here on four paws as opposed to two legs. From there, it was relatively easy to follow the smell of blood off into the lightly wooded area that separated one tobacco farm from its neighbor.

As I tracked them further, I found myself at a small farm somewhat west of the public house. Someone had cleared trees back a ways so the house could be built nearly flush with the treeline. Thick black smoke billowed into the night sky from behind the house, obscuring the stars as it carried the scents of the pack, pine, and burning flesh along the wind.

They were burning Abner's body.

I didn't dare interrupt their memorial, and the fatigue was becoming an unignorable pressure throughout my limbs. I headed downwind of them to find a hollow to sleep for the night. I barely managed to get the saddle off my horse before I slumped to the ground in a heap.

Better to offer my reparations and condolences in the full light of day anyway.

I woke to hooded dark eyes and long brown hair

studying me with crossed arms. He smelled of earthy tobacco, his scent sharp with anger.

"You've got a lot of nerve showing up here," he growled.

I nodded and put my hands up in a placating gesture. "I know, but I'm not here to fight."

"Won't make a difference to Matt. You'll be lucky if he doesn't kill you."

Which would be the opposite of my goal here.

He took a step back as I sat up.

"Matt's your alpha?"

He squinted at me. "No, Matt's the one whose face you caved in."

I took a deep breath and raked my hand through my hair. "Your alpha willing to have a chat?"

He nodded. "He wants to know why the bear is here. I'll take your horse."

He had already put the saddle back on the creature.

"Thanks… "

"Sampson."

"Thank you, Sampson." I tossed the saddlebag over my shoulder and followed him.

He was gentle with my horse, though his gait was stiff with restrained anger. Anger I could hardly blame him for. Anger I was sure to meet from the rest of his pack.

I inhaled deeply of the morning air and controlled my emotions. This was a pack in pain. Worse, I was to blame for their pain. I was responsible for their loss. It would not do to provoke or disrespect them on their own territory in such a state.

As we approached the house, Sampson split off to the left, and I continued to the door.

The alpha threw open the door as my foot hit the step, his nails biting into the wood.

"Tell me why I shouldn't kill you where you

stand." His warm scent was as sharp with anger as Sampson's had been.

I was impressed with his restraint. I had expected him to rush me.

"I'd really rather it not come to that," I said. "Because I'm not sure you could."

His chest puffed at the challenge, and his heartbeat quickened.

I probably shouldn't have said that last part, true or not. It did not matter to me that they had started it, nor that they had misidentified what I was before being shown. I had killed one of theirs for a simple mistake they had made, one they had no way of knowing the better of until it was too late, and that was enough.

I raked a hand through my hair and looked at the alpha's chest. "But more importantly," I hurried to add, "because, despite all appearances, we are on the same side."

I looked at him then. He had his fists on his hips, taking up as much space as he could in the doorway. The other two pack members lurked behind him, their arms crossed as they waited on the outcome.

This could turn into a shit show, as it had at the public house, if I wasn't careful.

I took a deep breath and gingerly placed the saddlebags next to the steps of the door before meeting the furious gaze of the alpha. My eyebrows shot up in surprise.

His eyes were the unmistakable gold of a born wolf.

There weren't many of those around these days. I blinked to refocus on the matter at hand.

I took a deep breath. "And because I sincerely regret the damage I have caused to your pack."

He studied me for a moment, one eyebrow raised as he worked the muscles in his jaw. "How could we possibly be on the same side? You killed one of mine!"

"He was like a brother to me!" Matt lunged from the shadows behind the alpha's left shoulder. His canines were pronounced, telling me all I needed to know about how ready he was to try to tear me apart.

Which was more than fair, truth be told.

The alpha sharply raised his hand, pointer finger extended.

Matt stopped cold.

Peeling his gaze from mine, the alpha looked hard at his packmate. There were scars where I had smashed in his face. What used to be a brown eye had healed overnight to milky white, while the other shone nearly as gold as his alpha's despite the shadows.

The glass must've really put up a fight on its way out. Or else there was still some wedged deep enough into the eye socket that there was no getting it out.

I wondered if he was even able to see out of that clouded eye. Guilt filled my throat with bile, and my heart pounded as I took another steadying breath. Cool heads would keep this from getting ugly.

"I cannot replace what was lost," I said, spreading my hands, "and I would not insult you by offering money. The church created me, just as they created your kind."

A deeper resentment than simple anger sat in the alpha's furrowed brow and half snarl. "We do not serve the church."

It seemed the alpha found something personally offensive about even the suggestion that he could. Interesting. Still, something better left unasked about, at least for now. Too much pain and anger now. Too much *justified* pain and anger.

I shook my head. "Nor do I. Never again. And

while I'd rather they not have a way to track and find me again, certain debts are more important than anonymity."

The alpha crossed his arms and waited for me to continue. The knuckles of his balled fists cracked.

I swallowed around my shame. "I offer you three favors. Whatever you ask of me, whenever you ask it. One for the loss, one for the damage, and one for the pack."

It was all I could think of to offer. All I truly had that was of any real value. I think he understood the gravity of my offer. I hoped he did.

He studied me for a moment, thinking. "How can you be sure I would not exploit such favors?"

Hmm. He was likely younger than I gauged him to be. Older creatures seemed to understand the gravity of favors offered by elder things. At least the concept had distracted him from the immediacy of his anger.

"Because it is not in your nature," I replied. "Just as it is not in mine. Your pup pushed hard against a creature he knew nothing about, and that creature reacted poorly to such provocation." I pressed my hand to my chest and bowed my head. "I shall never make that mistake again, and I sincerely thank your packmate for teaching an old bear new tricks."

Like making sure I let the bear roam free more often. Something I should have known already, but which had not been an issue until now.

His warm scent dulled, blending with the rest of his pack's once again. Apparently my submissive posture spoke to his alpha nature. Well, good. I kept my head bowed, though I was ready for refusal and a fight. I wanted neither, but I had learned long ago to wait out wolves. I should have done so at the public house.

"I will give one of your favors to him," he said finally. "The one you damaged."

I looked up and glanced between him and the wolves behind him.

"I don't want his damn favor," Matt barked, his canines still elongated. He folded his arms stiffly across his chest.

The alpha rounded on him, his scent sharpening again as he poked a finger against Matt's chest, above his crossed arms.

"You will keep it until such time that you need it, Matthew." He spoke in a quiet, deliberate tone that left no room for argument as his power washed through me, though it was ineffectual.

Matt, however, ducked his head and looked away.

Taking a deep breath to collect himself, the alpha turned back to me. "I shall keep the other two favors for the pack. There is nothing you can do for us now, we shall simply have to see what restitution your offer becomes."

"As you wish, Alpha."

I looked to where Sampson stood with my horse and again marveled that such beasts managed to stay calm around us. Some things never ceased to impress me.

"I am traveling on from this place," I said, "but I will send word to you when I arrive where I am headed. From there, I shall keep in touch so that you can reach me when you have need of me. I would not punish your pack with the burden of my presence through such fresh grief."

Sampson brought my horse closer, his grip on the reins firm. He and the alpha watched as I picked up my saddlebags and tossed them over my horse's back. The tendons in Sampson's neck strained at the strength with which he clenched his jaw.

The alpha crossed his arms again, but this time, his hands remained relaxed as I swung myself up and into the saddle.

He looked at me as I settled my weight. "What should I call you, should I decide to? Pack-killer hardly seems appropriate."

"If that is the worst you could call me, I'd be grateful for it." I smiled at him. "But Kristos is my given name. And I pray you do call on me, Alpha, that I may prove to you we are on the same side. If you would be kind enough as to give me your name, I shall be sure any missives from you are given immediate attention."

The alpha nodded. "Tobias Sheppard."

FOUR

TOBIAS SHEPPARD WAITED a full fifty years to cash in his first favor. Long enough that I thought he'd forgotten about it, though I had dutifully kept him apprised of my whereabouts, as promised. But during the American Revolution, when the dogmatic packs of the Anglican church threatened the Native American packs, he sent word through war-torn pre-America to ask for my assistance.

"The church sent over a handful of packs that are larger in number than we usually see," he explained. "They put one pack in charge of the rest, and that pack's alpha is far stronger than I. They aren't taking no for an answer, Kristos."

"And you need my help to make them see reason."

"You said you turned from the church. You know the pressure they'll use. I watched my family die thanks to the church's inaction. My pack is standing up for the other packs here. Don't let me watch them die too. Are we on the same side or aren't we?"

I hesitated. My history with the church was rocky enough that if they realized I was still around, they could—and likely would—make my life very uncomfortable until I came to heel.

But then I remembered Abner, and my hesitation melted into impassive resolve. There was a debt to be paid, and Tobias Sheppard held the note.

"We are."

It turned out the church wanted more than the subjugation and conversion of the natural packs in the New World. They wanted virtual dominion over the new land. And they were willing to fight their own brethren to get it. The vampires reveled in such violence, of course, and took every opportunity they could to strike at the forces in the night. The wolf packs of what would later be America were fighting on two fronts, and they were weary and worn for all the good it did.

It was a wonder the human world didn't learn even then about the things that go bump in the night. I suspect willful ignorance was at play.

So, we set up a meeting with the lead alpha. The plan was to try to reason with the church packs. They were good wolves, fighting the same good fights against the spread of the earthbound demons that the packs here did. There was no need for violence.

Except the meeting was an ambush. To the church alpha, it was an opportunity to take down who he saw as the lead alpha of the colonial packs. A werebear had not been part of his calculations. It never was, really. So, when he attacked Sheppard, I bashed his skull in.

It left us with no choice but to take out the church packs. And their organization was top-notch. We had to use guerrilla strike tactics to take the church alphas down one by one. We fed information to the sheep we could find to get the vamps where we needed them to be, setting up fights between the church alphas and the local coteries while Sheppard's pack distracted the rest of the church pack members.

It was brutal work that I am far from proud of, but at least there were plenty of bloodsuckers dying too.

In short order, what remained of the church packs picked up and went home. Or at least they went somewhere else.

Well, most of them did.

When all was said and done, Sheppard's pack was more than a handful of wolves larger, he was certain of our alliance, and we went our separate ways.

FIVE

IT WAS NEARLY 150 years before I heard from Sheppard again. America had finally joined the first World War that spring, and the vampires' numbers had been rising almost exponentially while the men of America were off fighting on distant shores.

A pair of elder vampires overseas must have seen that as their opportunity. There were fewer people here, and most of them women, whom they considered the weaker sex. Hell, their own government hadn't even granted them the right to vote yet.

When those elder vampires arrived, they immediately got to work organizing the scattered vampire coteries, amassing power and entrenching themselves in society. Sheppard must have felt it was his personal duty to stop them. I remember having such zeal.

"All those years ago," he said, "you told us our pack hadn't seen real vampires. That none had come here yet. Well, the heavy hitters are here. And now the pack will discover for themselves what you already know. Help us stop them."

That was a request easily fulfilled.

Or so I thought.

I had grown complacent in the new lands of

lesser vampires. I had forgotten how cunning and ruthless they could be.

It took months of dismantling government conspiracies to even get close to the power couple. Conspiracies that kept women working in dangerous conditions and being fed upon as thanks for their hard work. Regulations on textile factory safety were few, thanks to machinations of the coterie within city council and the state legislative boards. Between mayors on the payroll of the vampires and state representatives being blackmailed into cooperation, the vampires—Nicholaus and Emelina—could do virtually anything they wanted within their factory walls. Factories were rarely inspected, at least the ones they controlled, and when they were, the inspectors were easily paid off. The only way we found any of it was to track the money, a task made that much harder as it became clear they also had local mob bosses in their pockets, laundering any cash they came by.

Even then, the vampires dared the wolves to make themselves public, to show the world what lurks in the shadows of their cities.

Beyond the humans under their thumb, Nicholaus and Emelina had amassed a truly impressive number of minions. The vampires in their immediate coterie numbered close to forty, with another 25 or so within the region whose names were regularly heard in our investigations.

And in the final push to get to Nicholaus and Emelina, the forty in their immediate coterie almost wiped out Sheppard's pack. Worse, so many sheep— otherwise innocent humans—fought and died for the creatures that would drink them dry for the pleasure of it. It was always worse when the sheep fought. It was a dirty tactic that took a toll on the morale of every werewolf forced to put one down.

Sheppard played the part of distraction while I

fought the elder vampires, keeping the rest of the co-terie occupied with his pack. It had been a long time since I had fought anything so old, and these elders were smart. Not only did they force us to confront them at night, when we could not possibly ambush them, we were forced to fight them on their own turf —their main textile factory by the docks.

Nicholaus and Emelina kept to the shadows as I entered the factory, taunting me with threats of how they would flay me alive or fuck atop my bloody re-mains. And then one rushed past me, slicing into my shoulder and dashing away. Then the other did the same from the other direction as I spun to face the first attack. They were fast, and even with the won-derful night vision being a werebear granted me, I could not track them nearly so well as I would have liked in the factory. I tried to catch one on the next pass, but all I managed was to grab my own shoulder as the wound closed. My fingers came away bloody, and there was a quiet slurp that followed.

"Oh, Nicholaus," Emelina said in a sultry voice. "This one is a truly delightful delicacy!"

Another dashing slice from the shadows.

"Mmm," Nicholaus murmured. "Unlike any werewolf we've tasted."

Got 'em.

The next dash brought the head of one right into my waiting grip, and I smashed Nicholaus' body into the ground over and over until it was like flinging around a rag doll.

"That's because I'm not a werewolf," I said, tearing the head from Nicholaus' limp body.

Emelina flew into a rage, dashing around the fac-tory, starting fires around the outer walls. The fine dusting of lint over virtually every inch of the factory caught in a flash. But she must have known it was over already. With all the flickering light, it became that much easier to track her, and when she tried to dash at me again from the last remaining shadowy spot large enough to hide her, I simply twisted her head from her body like the cap from a tube of toothpaste.

Their deaths sang in my veins in a way not entirely unlike Longinus' death, and I slept for days afterward as Sheppard mourned those he'd lost in the fight.

Still, we had succeeded. The elder vampires fell.

Some of the sheep from that night became werewolves, and though most of those lost their minds at the next full moon, some did not. That was how Sheppard's pack became the consummate pack for those who never wanted to be werewolves in the first place. A place for those who didn't belong elsewise.

I only wish we had figured out then how deep the vampires had entrenched themselves in American politics.

SIX

SINCE I HADN'T EVEN STARTED DRIVING until after dark, I only managed to get to Lafayette—barely more than two hours along my drive—before I needed to make a rest stop.

My problem is sleeping. I'm not built for long-haul stalk-and-chase runs. I'm built to wait out my prey and expend my energy in bursts.

Fighting makes me incredibly tired.

Driving is almost as bad.

I have to stop every few hours and sleep off the highway hypnosis. Thankfully, I can sleep anywhere, including the cab of my truck at a highway rest stop.

Which I did.

For hours.

I made it past Shreveport on the next leg, but by then, I needed more than just a rest stop nap, and the squat little roadside motel's 'Vacancy' neon was like a shining beacon in the dying light of sunset. I didn't care that the paint was peeling and the doors were rusty around the locks and handles. It was a place to sleep.

As I pulled into the parking lot, my phone dinged. I shut off the ignition and looked at the notification. Kleinenburg's client had accepted my draft for their necklace and signed the contract. I threw my bag over my shoulder and checked the balance of my account as I headed to the office. The deposit was paid. Good.

The office looked like it hadn't seen a renovation since it was built in the seventies, and it stank of vampires.

Fuck.

And I was too tired to give a shit about it.

So, I went to the front desk where the very human clerk—a sheep, by the smell of it—checked me in and gave me my room key. It was an actual metal key on a ring with a plastic hang tag. And it looked to be about as old as the decor in the office.

I speared the gaunt, big-haired blonde with a look. She looked like she had one foot in the grave already.

"Be sure to tell your night manager this room is best left alone tonight. How you folks run this place is your business, but this sleeping bear is best left un-poked."

She blinked vapid blue eyes at me. "I'm certain I don't know what you're referring to, sir."

Of course not. Not that it mattered, her tone gave her away. She was lying.

The vampires here were likely to drain her to within an inch of her life tonight and then shove her back at the desk in the morning. Rinse and repeat until she died.

I rubbed my face and sighed as I headed to the room she'd assigned me. Easy enough to find since all the doors faced the parking lot.

I should have gotten back in my truck and driven the next handful of miles to get to the next roadside motel. I even thought about it as I went back to my truck to get my kit. Though I was tired, sleep was not yet threatening to take me.

But fuck it. I had a commission to work on anyway. Besides, if they did attack, well that would at least reduce the number of vamps able to prey on whatever poor travelers decided this sketchy-as-hell motel was worth stopping at. And if they didn't, I got a good night's sleep out of the deal. Win win.

I locked the door and turned on the TV. It only got the local stations, but at least the nightly news was on. Apparently, the next county over was reeling from some wild animal attack that had left two dead.

Probably vampires, not wild animals.

I shook my head as I headed for the shower. The water never really got hot, but that wasn't exactly surprising. I just wanted to rinse off before getting to work on the commission.

I threw on a pair of pants after my shower and opened the large tackle box I kept my jeweler supplies in. I loosely tied my hair back with an old strip of leather and pulled the little round table closer to the lamp for better light. After pulling the sketchbook from my bag, I opened it to the draft I had made for Kleinenburg's client as I sat in one of the worn wooden chairs. I then pulled one of two velvet pouches from within my kit, and poured the contents into my hand: twelve round opals, matched in size and color, and each about the size of a small blueberry. Setting the pouch down, I placed the opals on top and got to work neatly setting each onto gold wire. The work had a peaceful sort of repetition to it.

It's a good thing I give myself plenty of lead time to get a piece finished. A multiple-day road trip to Colorado would have otherwise set me back, but Harold Kleinenburg was good at his job. With the right combination of word-of-mouth marketing and simulated rarity, he'd made sure my pieces were in high demand these days. Which meant clients were willing to wait—and pay top dollar—for one of barely a handful of my exclusive, one-of-a-kind items designed and delivered each year. It made life in the very capitalist modern America much easier.

This piece would bring in the most yet, though its design was simple elegance.

I worked until I had all the opals on their own individual bits of gold wire, and then carefully placed them back in their pouch. Once they were settled in their place, I neatly put the rest of my tools and supplies away and locked the case. It was a good place to stop on the project, and the repetition had allowed the sleepiness to take hold of me.

I didn't bother getting under the scratchy blanket of the squeaky bed. I wasn't cold.

But as I reached to turn off the light, the lock on the door to my room clicked open.

I looked at the clock on the nightstand. Just past eleven. Well after full dark. The night manager hadn't gotten my warning, of course.

"Now's your chance to close the door and walk away," I grumbled, resettling into the lumpy pillow as I clicked off the light. Even if they attacked, I wouldn't need the light to kill them.

"One wolf does not scare us," the vampire hissed as she burst through the door. She was a lanky thing with greasy brown hair that fell in her face.

Dumbass.

Sometimes, it was a real pain in the ass to be the only werebear left.

I kicked out of bed toward her as she rushed me, machete held high. She buried it into the spot where my neck met my shoulder, slicing along my left arm as it went, but I already had my hands on her head. With a satisfying crack, I snapped her neck and dropped the body to my left as I continued toward the first of her friends.

Sweeping my right arm low, I took out the legs of

the next vampire, which happened fast enough to bring him almost horizontal, and as gravity kicked in, I smashed my elbow into his face, driving him to the ground. When he landed, his head was little better than a meat-and-bone pudding.

The third vampire, who had come in behind the first two, managed to get a good hit into my collarbone with his machete, hard enough it would have fractured in a werewolf. I grunted at the pain as I wrapped his arm, trapping it against me. I reached across his body, grabbing his left shoulder, and wrenched it hard to my left as I threw him over me and into the far wall.

It left his dismembered arm on the ground next to me. I picked up the machete he had been holding as I stalked over to where he was shouting in pain, and jammed the blade deep through his face, burying it into the drywall behind his head.

He stopped shouting then.

The door to the adjoining room burst open and two more vampires entered my room, brandishing the same kinds of machetes their friends had. Because of course they did. I rolled my eyes. This fucking coterie must've bought out the local hardware store's stock.

Wrenching the machete hard to my left, I snapped the neck of the one I'd pinned to the wall. It popped his head clean from his body.

I looked at the new arrivals and waggled the head of their buddy on the machete at them. They looked at each other and ran out the door they'd just come through.

Good. Fuck 'em.

I can't kill every fucking bloodsucker I come across. If I did, I'd be fighting until the end of time. And I'd draw a hell of a lot of attention to myself.

I looked at the gaunt bodies strewn around my

motel room. These vamps were starved. Business clearly wasn't booming along this stretch of highway. Three wouldn't have even been enough to take a wolf, but five would have if they'd coordinated better. They must've been young still.

I collected the bodies of the dead vampires and brought them to the east side of the building. I hid them between the dumpsters there and threw the machetes into the giant metal container. The morning sun would turn the corpses to ash, and no one would be the wiser.

I stopped at the office on my way back to my room. It was empty and stank even more of vampire than it had earlier in the day.

Guess the night desk clerk was among the bodies next to the dumpster. No surprise that the vampires themselves would cover the night shift. Hopefully, the vapid blonde was getting what rest she could instead of lying dead in one of the other rooms.

I pushed a dark, wet lock of my hair from my face. I needed another shower, and I sure as hell wasn't taking one in a smashed up room covered in blood. So I fished around the drawers behind the front desk until I found the keys for the other rooms. I looked at the map taped to the drawer bottom. Twenty-seven was the room closest to the office.

Good enough.

I grabbed the key for room twenty-seven and turned to leave, but a black and white TV on a desk in a side room caught my eye. The screen was divided into quarters, each section showing a different view of the motel's footprint.

Security cameras.

Fuck.

Of course.

It was a vamp-run motel, but those fuckers were likely to have their fingers in every pie they could. If there were any left that hadn't been stupid enough to confront me in my room, I wouldn't put it past them to send footage to the police and pressure them to stop my cross country trek.

As I watched the screen, it switched to a view with only two of the four quarters filled, the other two blank. It showed the front desk and this security room. I forced myself not to look at where the camera was, and bent to trace the wires to the bland beige box that housed the machine recording the footage. And then I smashed the box with my fist, taking the tape and the hard drive with me as I headed back to my room.

They had put me in room thirteen. I hadn't even paid attention to it when I checked in.

Those fucking cliché idiots probably marked that room for easy prey. I sucked on my teeth and shook my head as I shoved the bits from the security machine into my bag. Throwing the strap over my shoulder, I grabbed my tackle box and the room keys.

Over in room twenty-seven, I showered and passed out in the bed until the dawn light woke me.

I took my bag and kit to the truck and headed for the office.

Sure enough, the big haired blonde was on duty again this morning, looking even worse than she had the night before, if that was possible. The office was otherwise empty. Her sunken blue eyes met mine and widened. She glanced to her left, the direction of the security room, and then back at me, her heart pounding.

I flashed her a predatory grin as I placed the keys to both rooms on the counter. I usually play nice with the human-folk, but this particular one had vexed me.

"Room thirteen will need a deep clean," I said,

glaring at her as I wrinkled my nose in a half snarl. "It had a vermin problem last night that got a little messy."

She shrank in the chair and tried not to look at me.

"And I suspect you'll need a new night manager," I added through gritted teeth as I turned to walk away.

Saving sheep is not my problem. Certainly not ones who tried to set me up. They'll either survive or they won't. And even if I killed all the vampires of that coterie, there would have been nothing I could do for the madness that follows as the feed addiction wears off.

SEVEN

ROMAN EMPIRE, PRE-HARVEST 170

BACK WHEN I *wasn't* the only werebear left on the planet, there were scores of us. My brothers. The budding Catholic church sent us out on missions in squads of three or four, which explained why they liked our successors' tendency toward pack so much. As it was, we didn't really coordinate so much as we were wild barbarians that simply didn't kill each other when it came to fighting vampires.

But damn if we weren't effective. The church was beyond pleased with their creation.

If the church got wind of a vampire coterie somewhere, they'd pick a group of us and send us out. We'd get to where they were, drink wine and break bread like we were at mass, and pray the last rites for those we were destroying—and for the lives these night-walking demons had already taken. We nearly always waited until full noon to be sure the vampires were down and resting, and to ensure they'd have to be careful around windows and the light of day. And then we'd wipe them out.

It was glorious.

Once a coterie was cleared, we'd report back to the church with whatever we found there. It was routine. How many vampires? How many dead? What sort of structure had they chosen for a stronghold? How many humans were killed in the fray?

There were always humans killed in the fray.

Innocents who had fallen under the influence of the powers of the vampires.

Initially, we didn't see much in the way of feeder humans—just vampires and dead bodies. But somewhere around fifty years after our creation, vampires learned to control who they turned, and we started to see them keeping humans like livestock. Once we started seeing human sheep, we had to bring them back to the church after clearing a coterie. The madness of withdrawal from the creature feeding from them was a curious thing, but nothing worse than the church had seen from those addicted to wine or the milk of the poppy. The church healed them, gave them purpose. They became nuns and bishops and acolytes of the church.

And then, finally, the church found him.

Longinus.

The Roman soldier who had speared Jesus in his moment of doubt on the cross.

The first of the night-walking demons.

He had caused immeasurable amounts of chaos, turning everyone he sunk his fangs into, and draining dry whatever livestock he came across. The sheer devastation caused by that single creature was absolutely astounding.

I never once questioned how the church learned of his whereabouts. It didn't matter. He was in Macedonia, and I was granted the indescribable honor of being among the bears sent to kill the first vampire. They sent seven of us. This vampire was the oldest of them all. Surely he would be stronger than the others we had faced.

They weren't wrong.

We found him in the hovel of the last family he'd

killed. He didn't have human sheep. The goats and cattle were bled dry, their desiccated remains drawing flies and scavenging creatures. No vampires kept him company. And this family's hovel reminded me too much of my own from before I had become a creature of the church. Remembering the deaths of my family fueled my rage at this vile creature. We had not planned to wait for the sunrise; we didn't dare lose him.

Others had seen him fight through shadows, appearing where he hadn't been before. He didn't wait for us to come to him. Once he knew we were there, he bolted through the shadows of full night to meet us. The previous reports were true. He fought with a fierce zeal that bordered on madness, using a farmer's scythe to decapitate one of my brothers before we'd even realized he was there. I was still reeling from the shock of coming against something so quick and quiet and strong when he cut a second one of my brothers effectively in half from behind.

The church had not misjudged his strength.

Two more of my brothers fell as we forced him out of the hovel and into the pasture, where he had no cover to hide behind. Which left me and two others. The fight was a blur, fueled by the rage of the deaths of my brothers. But I still recall the moment I crushed his head between my claws, his teeth still sunk into my fur. My heart filled with purpose in that moment, and the unbridled elation sang through my body like a plucked harp string as the last vestiges of his life left him.

He may have been the first vampire to walk the Earth, but I ended his reign of terror.

If only that had been enough to stop all of them.

EIGHT

IT WAS ONLY about two and a half hours from Shreveport to Dallas, and the morning sun was warm and calming on the back of my neck through the rear windshield of the cab.

Too warm and calming.

Like the fucking highway hypnosis.

Dammit.

I took the next exit and wound my way into the parking lot of a diner, hoping breakfast would help distract me from the ridiculousness of my biology. The werewolves had it easy. They didn't fatigue like I did.

The diner was a hole in the wall place with red sparkle vinyl booths and shiny steel tables, but the food smelled good. Inside, there was one other couple, seated in one of the booths. I went to the counter. No need to take up a booth when it's only me. The waitress brought me coffee and handed me a menu as I sat on a stool, but the morning news on the TV in the corner had grabbed my attention.

They were playing a video, shot from someone's cell phone. It was a little grainy, but it was definitely a vampire being assaulted by a werewolf in an alleyway. I could tell by the way they moved. The wolf pulled the bloodsucker back into the club he'd left before the video ended, but there was no mistaking those two for what they were.

It made me glad I'd taken the tape and hard drive from the motel outside Shreveport.

Humans may have been ignorant of the creatures that protected them for centuries, but these young pups were getting careless. Technology was making the world smaller, and the population of wolves had been growing, for the most part. It was simply a matter of time before the humans and werewolves and vampires had to come to terms with a world where they all coexist. Except war would happen first.

War always happened first.

And the way humans wage war is so much uglier than the war the wolves have had against the vampires. Maybe I'd be lucky enough to pass before that happened.

When the waitress wandered back toward my side of the counter, I ordered the biggest breakfast they offered, and added a slice of apple pie as well. She looked over my shoulder at my truck like she expected to see someone else join me.

I smiled at her. "It's just me."

She waggled her pen at me. "Y'know, my ex husband used to eat like that. Something about breakfast like a king, lunch like a prince, dinner like a pauper."

"I've heard that adage. How'd it work out for him?"

She shrugged as she passed the slip of paper with my order to the kitchen. "He lost a buncha weight and ran off with my cousin. Turns out he was gay the whole time."

I whistled. "Sometimes it takes folks a while to figure that out."

She put a fist on her hip as she rolled her eyes.

"Woulda been nice if he'd done it before he married me. But I'm glad he's happy now at least. We spent way too much time fightin' anyway."

I nodded as she wandered off to care for the other diners.

She watched me after bringing my order, clearly doubtful I could eat it all. It was three plates piled high with pancakes, sausage, eggs, toast, and bacon, plus a side bowl for the grits, all told. Anyway, that doubt told me a lot about a place. For one, it meant she hadn't seen any werewolves come through her diner. Their appetites rival mine, except they almost exclusively crave meat. It also told me there probably weren't any vampires around either, as wolves tend to follow hot on the heels of vampires. At least, they do in relatively populated areas. Odds are good that the motel outside of Shreveport could have kept up its operations for a good long while as long as they didn't make waves.

But starved vampires make mistakes.

Mistakes make waves.

She whistled when I cleaned the plate... well, plates, really. But she still brought me my slice of apple pie. And here I was sure she'd forgotten it.

"Certainly haven't heard that accent 'round these parts," she said. "Where you from, anyway?"

I smiled around a bite of pie. "Little bit of everywhere. I spent a lot of time in Europe before coming 'across the pond' as it were."

"Well you sure can pack it away," she said as she handed me the check. "You must be active as hell."

I smiled at her. "I've just always been a big eater." I handed her enough cash to cover the food and a nice tip. I never skimp on tipping wait staff. I drank the last of my coffee and headed back to my truck.

The last time I had driven through the Dallas-Fort Worth metroplex was in the middle of the night, and it only took about an hour and a half. I knew daytime would be different, but it shouldn't take that much more time.

As it turns out, if you hit the tail end of morning rush hour just right, and some asshole causes an accident that shuts down two lanes of traffic on the freeway, it can take you four goddamn hours to get from one side of the metroplex to the other.

The breakfast had at least distracted me enough to let me stay awake as I crawled my way through the sprawling cityscape. But I had to pull into a rest stop on the far side of Fort Worth for another nap before continuing on. Which meant I didn't even get to Abilene until after dark.

And I needed a beer after that bullshit drive across the metroplex. Not that it was going to do much for me, but there was a peaceful sort of ritual to getting a fresh beer from the draft at a good bar. Thank God for technology making it easy to find one along your driving route.

My truck fit right in at the lot of the bar I'd chosen, and country music blared from inside. Cigarette smoke assaulted my nose as I entered.

There were pool tables set in parallel along the right side of the establishment, and a wood-paneled bar stretched nearly the full length of the left side.

"Knock it off, Chad!" A pretty college co-ed giggled as she pushed a drunk guy away so she could line up her shot.

I sat down at the bar and ordered a draft beer. I tried to ignore the couple at the pool table.

"Come on, Ash, let's get out of here so I can show you around *my* stick!"

Drunk assholes are not my problem.

I took a slow sip of my beer. They weren't the only ones at the bar anyway, not even the only ones playing pool. They were, however, the ones I watched in the mirror above the bar.

"No, I wanna finish the game." She giggled at him again, but there was an undercurrent of fear in the sound.

I couldn't hear her heartbeat over the twang of the country music that Chad kept trying to get her to dance to. My guess? It was pounding in her chest.

I drained the last of my beer.

"You know I'm gonna beat you at it like I always do!"

"So show me what I'm doing wrong!" It was clear on her face in the mirror—she knew the mistake of that request even as she made it.

But Chad jumped on it, thinking entirely too much with the head between his legs. He came around behind her as she lined up her next shot and grabbed at her breast while grinding his hips against her ass.

"Come on, Chad! Stop. Help me line up a good shot." She didn't giggle that time. Instead, fear had crept into her words.

He licked her neck. "But I wanna line up *my* shot."

So much for a peaceful beer.

Maybe I was tired and grumpy from the ridiculous drive across the metroplex.

Or maybe I was uppity and on edge knowing if I didn't get to that *purgatum* before too long, she was gonna be hung out to dry. Her pack was no match for what the church could bring to bear on her if they learned about what she was.

Or maybe—just maybe—I didn't like seeing a lady get harassed when she'd been clear about her refusal.

Whichever it was, I drained the last of my beer

and ordered two more. When they came, I paid and took them over to Chad and Ash.

Up close, she looked like a cornered rabbit. I could finally smell her fear through the cigarette smoke. Chad probably scared her even when he wasn't drunk and trying too aggressively to get in her pants.

Chad, on the other hand, had the smooth look of a predator, though he was neither vampire or were-wolf. He was just an average, run-of-the-mill horny jackass.

I offered one of the beers to him. "Sounds like the lady's not too into what you're layin' down. Maybe it's time to cut your losses."

"What the hell do you know, old man?"

He could barely focus on me, but he slapped at the hand offering the beer. He must've expected it to hit the ground. When it didn't, he hit it again, this time clearly aiming to have it pour all over me. He was unsuccessful at that as well, and I just stared at him.

Recognizing help when it arrived, Ash scooted closer to me.

Smart girl.

He squinted and blinked at me before looking back at the scared co-ed. "This guy your uncle or something, Ash? What the hell?"

"She doesn't know me, Chad," I said, keeping my tone low. "I think it's time you left your lady friend here alone for the night."

Shock slammed into his expression. "What the *fuck*?! How the hell do you know my name?"

He ripped the pool cue from Ash's hand, causing her to shift closer to me yet again. He brandished it at me like it was a baseball bat. "I'll kick your ass, you stalker!"

Not fuckin' likely. Maybe if he was packing an

actual rocket launcher in his pants. But his too-tight jeans told me that was out of the question.

Ash continued her slow trek around the pool table toward me and away from Chad.

"It's not something worth fighting over, man. Just leave the lady alone."

That was when he lunged in and swung at me with the pool cue.

I didn't duck. I didn't dodge. Hell, I didn't even feel it as the stick broke across the side of my face. I simply stared impassively at Chad and took a sip of the beer in my other hand.

I placed the beer I had offered him down on the edge of the pool table before pulling the broken stub of the pool cue from his white-knuckled grip. "This is me calm, Chad. You won't like me when I'm angry. *No one* likes me when I'm angry. Call a friend, get a ride home, and listen to your lady when she says no."

His face paled at my tone. I took another slow sip of my beer as I maintained eye contact with him.

Chad's unfocused eyes darted around the bar, looking for friends or anyone he recognized. Maybe he hoped someone else would step in and help him. It didn't matter. The rest of the people at the bar were forcefully ignoring us. He ran a shaky hand through his spiky brown hair.

"Man, fuck this," he said finally. "I'll find easier girls at Jason's party Friday night anyway." He turned on his heel and stalked out the door.

Ash grabbed the beer from the side of the pool table as he left. As soon as he was gone, the fear faded from her scent.

I bent to pick up the other half of the pool cue from the floor and took it over to the bar.

"Sorry for the broken stick, man." I pulled a handful of twenties from my pocket and laid them on the bar alongside the broken pool cue. "Hopefully this'll help you guys buy a replacement or two."

The bartender nodded at me. "Normally, I'd kick someone out for causing that kind of a scene."

"Aw come on, Leo," Ash said, cutting me off before I'd even opened my mouth to reply. "He was just standin' up for a damsel in distress."

I raised an eyebrow at her as she tossed her coat over one of the barstools. The now much less afraid co-ed leaned against the bar next to me, close enough to smell the vanilla and floral of her perfume.

She tossed the big curls of her strawberry blonde hair over her shoulder and raised her glass at me. "Do heroes have names where you come from?"

I closed my eyes to keep from rolling them at her, but smiled. "Kris."

There was a lull between songs. Her heart still pounded like a cornered rabbit.

"Ashley." She clinked the bottom of her glass against the side of the one in my hand.

The bartender leaned toward me, "You cause any more trouble, Kris-"

"I hear you." I put my hands up in a placating gesture. "No more trouble. Never wanted any to begin with."

NINE

Ashley wore jeans that hugged every curve of her hips and thighs, and her shirt was unbuttoned down to her bra line, showing nearly all of her ample cleavage. One hell of a view. Despite the deplorable way he managed to express it, I had to admit Chad had good taste in women. She sat down on the barstool next to mine and rolled the glass of beer between her hands before taking a gulp.

"So Kris," she licked her bottom lip, pulling it between her teeth for a moment. "Where's a girl gotta go to hear more of that accent?"

Ladies love the accent.

"Europe, mostly." I smiled at her. "Not anywhere specific, but you'd hear bits of it in Italy, Spain, Bulgaria—"

She whistled. "Heroes get around."

I inclined my head at her as I sipped my beer.

"Thanks for gettin' that creep to leave." Her voice was almost too quiet to hear over the music.

"You're welcome," I said. "You'd do well not to talk to him anymore. Asshole doesn't know when to stop."

She shrugged as she rolled the glass of beer between her palms. "Do you?" Her beautiful hazel eyes met mine.

"Sure." I took another drink of my beer. "A lady says she wants your help getting better at a game, you help her, not grope her. And if a lady says stop, you get your damn hands off her."

She smiled and leaned in close to me, her voice dropping low. "And what if a lady says," her lips brushed my ear and her hand wrapped around the inside of my thigh, "take me home with you, hero? Lemme thank you properly?"

Wouldn't be the first time I took someone up on an offer like that. Though taking her to any kind of bed would be a bad idea, mine or otherwise. I'd made enough waves in this town as it was. But fuck if I didn't want to see what that body looked like laid bare beneath me.

It had been a while since I had something so pretty ready to go. And I'm generally not particularly reticent to take a person to bed, man or woman, no strings attached.

Still…

I took a deep breath. "I'm just passing through. I'll be gone by morning."

It was supposed to be a refusal.

She smirked at me and downed the last of her beer. "Even better." She found the bulge of my pants and pressed her palm to it.

I watched her in the mirror behind the bar, my gaze tracing the curves of her body as I downed the last of my beer. I savored the taste of it in my mouth, enjoying the view for perhaps a moment longer than I should have. Her hand hadn't left my lap, and I was hardening against her palm.

She met my eyes in the mirror, and her smirk turned into a flirty smile.

God, I'm a sucker for a good flirt.

Fuck it.

"Yeah, okay." I pulled some more cash from my pocket to cover a tip for the tender and left it on the bar under my glass.

She pulled on her coat and took my hand as I stood. She led me out the door, where I took over and led her to my truck. I moved my bag and box to the bed of the truck so she'd have room to sit in the cab. As I turned to go around to the driver's side, she pressed a hand to my chest. I stopped and watched her.

She spread her palm along my chest and slowly traced up to my jawline. She leaned in and pressed her mouth against mine, her tongue darting between my lips to get a taste of me. I returned the favor, pulling her gently against me. Her arm snaked around my neck and I lifted her into her seat, pressing her back and into the cab of my truck, where I abruptly pulled away from her, brushing along her cheek with my finger.

I wasn't about to fuck her in the parking lot.

She gave me a sly smile as I pointedly shut the door on her side of the truck. It was a sexy look for her, and I suspected she knew it.

I walked around to my side and looked at the map on my phone to find the closest motel. There was one a couple of blocks down the road from the bar.

Perfect.

She grabbed my hand once we were out of the parking lot and drew my finger into her mouth. She wrapped her tongue around my finger and slid it in and out of her mouth a few times before gently biting it.

Feisty little thing.

I smiled hungrily at her and almost missed the turn to the motel. I had to swerve into the parking lot from the far lane. The truck behind me pulled into the gas station next door.

"Lemme get checked in," I told her. "I'll be right back."

She unfastened a few more buttons of her shirt. "Don't take too long."

I smiled at her. "Of course not."

I am normally a very patient man, but it took entirely too fucking long for the lady at the front desk to check me in. Long enough that I watched the truck that had pulled into the gas station make a slow drive into the motel lot. As he creeped by my truck, I saw the spikey hair of the driver.

Chad.

That idiot followed me here. He must have been waiting in the parking lot of the bar. That asshole didn't know when to quit. With the roar of his truck's engine, he sped off down the lot and screeched onto the empty street.

I took a slow, deliberate breath and remembered Ashley's tongue on my finger and what she clearly wanted to do to other parts of me.

Fuck him.

He was just a guy.

An eternity later, the lady gave me the keycard for a room and I went back to the truck.

Ashley had her shirt completely open by the time I'd gotten back, and she'd shrugged her coat off.

"That asshole from the bar is likely to be back at an inconvenient time," I said to her.

She pouted at me. And in her red lace bra and tight blue jeans, it was the sexiest thing I'd seen in a while. "Then hurry to your room already." She reached for the bulge in my pants and squeezed gently along my shaft.

Plenty enough encouragement for me.

I drove us around to the side of the building

where my room was. Her mouth was on mine as I pulled the keys from the ignition, and I leaned back as she straddled my lap, running my hands along her thighs and up to the smooth skin of her lower back. As she pressed her body against me, I reached for her coat and shirt.

"God, you are warm," she said as she relaxed against me.

I smiled against her mouth. "Let's get you inside where we have a little more space."

She pulled back and twisted her lips into another flirty smirk as I pulled the coat onto her shoulders. She shifted her weight off my lap to let me open the truck door.

I moved my bag and jeweler's kit from the bed into the cab of the truck again before locking it. I'd worry about moving it into the room when I didn't have a hot little number to play with.

Once inside the room, she pressed her body against me and her mouth to mine. I locked the door and picked her up as she wrapped her arms around my shoulders. She let out a sultry little laugh as I plopped her down on the bed and pulled my shirt from my back. I waited for her to kick her shoes off before grabbing her hips and pulling her to me. She made a short squeak of a noise as I did, but it sounded mirthful, and her scent held no fear, just arousal. I peeled the jeans and red lace panties from her hips. The panties matched her bra. She reached for me, but I smiled at her and placed gentle pressure at her shoulder. She fell back as I hooked an arm around her waist and brought the junction of her thighs to my mouth.

"Oh shit, Kris," she moaned as my tongue lapped at her.

She tangled her hand in my hair and ground her hips against my mouth.

Slowly.

Then less so.

Building in intensity and speed, she arched her body as my tongue stroked her clit until, with a gasping moan, she came.

"Fuck," she said as the aftershocks washed over her. "I'm supposed to be thanking *you*."

My laugh was a low rumble and I flicked my tongue across her clit once more, reveling in the way her body jumped, before standing.

"So what's stopping you?"

That sexy smirk of hers returned as she sat up and reached for the fly of my jeans. I unhooked her bra and she dropped it to the ground as she freed my shaft from the confines of my pants. And then her warm mouth was on my dick and all rational thought left my mind.

Well, all except one.

Don't hurt her.

She was a human, and her body could not take the kind of force mine could.

I groaned my appreciation for her skill as I kept a loose grip on those strawberry blonde curls of hers and gently pumped my hips against her mouth. She took all of me down her throat without hesitation or complaint.

Repeatedly.

Until my elation brought me to my toes and my seed filled her mouth.

And then, with a self-satisfied smile, that delightfully sexy creature swallowed my cum.

As I gently pulled her to her feet, the rumble of a truck engine drew close to our end of the motel, shutting off as I kissed her.

Something crashed outside the window and I furrowed my brow as I looked over my shoulder. Curtains obscured the view into the parking lot.

"Hey stalker," a voice called, "you'll never please that whore!"

Human problems *really* aren't my problem. But this jackass was making himself my problem.

With a sigh, I turned and pulled the curtain aside. Sure enough, there was Chad, baseball bat in hand. And that fuckin' son of a bitch had smashed my tail light.

He also had three of his buddies in the bed of his truck, which was perpendicular to mine, blocking me into the parking spot.

Surprisingly, none of the guys in the truck bed held weapons.

I wiped at my face as I turned back to Ashley, who was hurriedly getting dressed, the fear back in her scent.

"Stay here," I told her, "lock the door behind me, and don't open it for that dick."

I picked up my pants and fished in the pockets till I found my wallet. I pulled a couple more twenties out, making a mental note to stop at an ATM on my way out of town.

"Here." I put the cash on the nightstand. "Call a cab to get you wherever you need to go. I'm gonna go deal with Chad, and then I'm gonna head out of town."

Her hazel eyes shot to mine. "You're just gonna leave?"

There was a pounding on the door as I pulled my jeans back on.

"Come on out and fight me like a man, stalker!"

I jerked my head toward the door. "Getting that asshole and his buddies gone will probably draw attention. Best if I don't stick around after that."

She threw her hands up in frustration as I picked up my shirt and shoes. "So much for thanking you."

I ignored her comment. "Do yourself a favor and

stop seeing him. And, for God's sake, be smart. Don't go out with assholes that scare you. It's just asking for trouble."

I didn't wait for her to say anything else. I opened the door and crowded Chad backward as I pulled the door closed.

Chad sized me up like he had in the bar as the lock clicked behind me.

"Looks like you and I need to have a little chat," he said.

"Not interested," I replied, shouldering past him to my truck. I tossed my shirt and shoes into the bed.

He followed close behind me. "You better be interested, asshole. You made me look like a fool in front of my girl."

I kept walking toward the back of my truck and eyed the busted tail light. "You made yourself look like a fool."

I took stock of the guys in the back of his truck. Curly red hair, lanky frame, human. Brown bowl cut, chiseled features, human. Bushy dark brown hair, tanned skin, human.

"And she isn't your girl," I added, huffing out an annoyed breath.

I stepped around to the back of his truck and grabbed the trailer hitch. Once my grip was sure, I lifted the rear wheels of the truck from the ground, sending the three guys in the back stumbling into one another.

"What the hell?!" Chad put his hands on his head as his eyebrows tried to join his hairline.

I pushed the truck forward and away from my tailgate, clearing the way for me to pull out of the parking spot. I dropped the backend of the truck to the asphalt with a thud. The three guys in the back toppled into a heap.

I turned and got in his face then. He was white as

the sheets of a fine hotel. Which this motel decidedly wasn't.

Grabbing the front of his shirt, I drove him backward toward the driver's side of his truck, his eyes like deer in the headlights. There, I roughly opened the door and shoved him into the seat. I slammed the door hard enough to make him flinch, but gently enough that I didn't do the damage that I really *wanted* to do to his truck.

I crossed my arms and waited. His heart slammed into the back of his sternum like it wanted to run away as bad as he did.

When he didn't move right away, I set my jaw and pointed forcefully down the road.

He took a shaky breath as comprehension dawned on him and pulled his keys from his pocket, starting the truck.

"She's outta your league anyway, Chad," I growled at him. "And so am I, for that matter."

He nodded with a shaky breath and I watched him drive away, his buddies now sitting in his truck bed.

I grabbed my shirt and shoes from the bed of my truck, tossed them in the cab, and drove away, leaving Ashley to sort out her own bullshit. Hopefully, she took my advice and called a cab for herself.

Human problems are *not* my problem.

TEN

THERE WEREN'T any auto parts stores open, so I was going to have to settle for replacing my tail light in the next little no-name town. And since small town cops tend toward boredom, it came as little surprise to me when red and blue lights flashed in my rearview mirror. Out-of-state plates might as well be dollar signs.

I huffed out a sigh as I pulled the truck onto the shoulder and slowed to a safe stop.

"License and registration," the officer said in a bored voice as I rolled my window down.

He was older, maybe his early fifties, with a bit of a gut. But he carried himself with the practiced air of someone who'd obviously been on the force the majority of his adult life.

I pulled out my wallet and made a show of digging through it. "Aw, hell. Must've left my license at the motel a few towns back."

"Mmhmm, registration?" More practiced authority.

I winced at him and patted the steering wheel gently, forcing respectfulness into my tone. "It's my buddy's truck, sir. Tobias Sheppard. I'm on my way to return it to him now."

"Where's that?"

"Colorado Springs, sir."

He rocked back on his heels and gestured toward the back of my truck. "You aware you have a tail light out, mister... ?"

"Smith, sir. Kris Smith." I hooked a thumb toward the broken tail light. "Yeah, I backed into a tree limb a town or two back. Plan on getting it replaced as soon as I pass a town that's got an auto parts store that's open."

He nodded, but his body language told me he was skeptical. "Uh huh. You got any other kind of identification on you, Mr. Smith?" He squinted at me. "A bank card with your photo perhaps?"

"I have a bank card," I pulled it from my wallet and offered it to him. "But there's no photo on it."

He took my card and looked at it for a moment. "So let me get this straight, Mr. Smith. Your buddy Tobias from Colorado Springs lends you his truck, brings it all the way to Texas for you—"

"Louisiana, sir," I said. "I picked it up from him in Louisiana."

"Mmhmm." He tapped the card against the palm of his other hand as he thought. "So Tobias brings his truck to you in Louisiana from Colorado Springs, just to have you drive it all the way back to him?"

He definitely didn't believe me.

I couldn't blame him, but there was no way he was going to believe the reason I didn't have a license or registration was because I was born before his grandparents were even a twinkle in his great-grandmother's eye.

I gave a small shrug. "Not sure how else I'd return the vehicle, honestly. You can call him if you'd like, sir. He had some paperwork drawn up like a sort of rental agreement. He emailed it to me, but I'm awful with that stuff. He can forward it to you if you'd like."

The officer narrowed his eyes at me. "Yeeeaaah, I'm gonna need you to step out of the vehicle for me, Mr. Smith."

"I'm sorry?"

"You're gonna need to come with me down to the station so I can verify this story of yours. I'm not callin' you a liar, you see. It's just you ain't got any proper identification on you, and you've admitted you're drivin' a truck that doesn't belong to you. I gotta run these plates and do my due diligence, y'see?"

I took a deep, steadying breath.

Just a guy doing his job.

"Of course, sir."

"Leave the keys there," he said, nodding to the steering wheel. "Keep your hands where I can see 'em. Get out of the truck slowly." His empty hand hovered over his gun.

I did as he said and let him pull my arms behind my back. He bound my wrists with zip ties and led me to his car, where he put me in the back seat. I fought against the part of me that wanted to rage and tear this car apart for even daring to suggest it could hold something like me captive as I watched him secure my truck, turning off the engine and locking the door. He radioed into the station as he came back to his car, alerting them he was en route with a suspect in custody.

Suspect.

I forced deep, steadying breaths into my lungs as I leaned back in the backseat.

I could have easily broken out, knocked out the officer—or even killed him—and simply driven off in my truck. A large part of me wanted to, begged to. I even considered it. But this guy was just doing his job. And as badly as I wanted to get to Colorado Springs post haste, I wasn't going to take an innocent down to get there a handful of hours sooner. I'd kick myself if that handful of hours meant the church caught up to the *purgatum*, but it had only been a few days since the phone call. I highly doubted the church could have caught wind of her and pulled a response together in such time.

"Hey Sharon," the officer said to the older lady behind the counter at the little run-down police station.

She looked over from the TV that was playing news up in the corner of the room, lifting her chin out of her hand, and nodded at the old cop. "Hey Jimmy." She eyed me. "Got yourself a looker there."

"Hmmph," Jimmy replied.

The officer placed me in a holding cell and removed the zip ties before trudging down the hallway to an office. There, he shut the door, obscuring my vision of him.

And apparently my hearing too. Sharon's damn TV was so loud it was clear she was going deaf as she got on in years. But even when I tried to listen past it, I heard nothing.

The office must've been soundproofed.

Interesting. That probably came in handy if things got rowdy in the holding cells.

I pressed my lips into a line and moved around in the cell until I could at least see what was on the news.

They had an analyst dissecting the cell phone footage from the other day. The one from the vampire and werewolf in the alleyway. Hell, that was just yesterday, wasn't it? Damn driving and sleeping had me mixed up.

"It's skillfully cut and doctored," the analyst explained. She was a tall woman in her mid-forties wearing a tailored white pantsuit. She gestured to a part of the video playing in slow motion on a screen behind her. "You see this blur here? That's where they've edited out the wire pulling this guy into the club."

She was a werewolf. I could see it in the way she moved, in the smooth way she shifted her weight on her feet. A wonder the pack in the metroplex had even managed to get her to go on live TV. This was probably a recast of the news segment from earlier that night. But at least the pups were getting out in front of the story, controlling the narrative before the vampires had a chance to do it for them.

"It's great work," she told the news anchor, spreading her palms wide. "Truly top-notch. But it would be silly to call this video anything more than a dramatization by a pair of talented creatives."

The door to the soundproofed office opened.

"Dammit," the officer who brought me in, Jimmy, spat. "Apparently, Colorado Springs checks out."

Sharon looked over at him. "You get a hold of the owner?"

"Yeah."

"And he corroborated the story?"

Jimmy ran a hand through his thinning hair. "Uh huh."

"He send his ID and the agreement?"

"Yeah." Jimmy's tone was annoyed now.

Sharon shook the eraser end of a pencil at him. "So you're gonna just hold this guy for a busted tail light and some forgetfulness? C'mon, Jimmy. He wouldn't've come along so willingly if he was full of shit."

Jimmy rolled his eyes and put his hands on his hips.

She sighed and leaned on the counter with one

arm, placing the other hand's fist against her hip. "We were about to hit the cutoff where we could go home and monitor calls from there, Jim. I'm tired. You're tired. Take the man back to his truck and let's call it a night."

The officer stood there thinking for a long moment before looking over at me.

"Promise I'll replace the tail light as soon as I find an auto parts store," I said. And it was true, I intended to do just that. "The motel probably mailed my ID to Colorado Springs, so I'll meet up with it when I drop off the truck."

Jimmy sucked on his teeth for a minute and stared at Sharon, who quirked an eyebrow at him.

Jimmy huffed and ran his hand through his hair again. "Yeah, alright."

He stepped over to the holding cell and unlocked it. I followed him wordlessly to his car and got in the backseat again for a drive back that was silent but for the road noise.

Once we got to my truck, he opened the back door for me again.

"Thank you, sir," I said, nodding to him. "Sorry to cause you the trouble."

"Mmhmm." He shut the door and jammed a finger toward the back of my truck. "Fix the tail light."

He turned as I passed him, and I felt him watching me as I got back into my truck. He'd left my bank card leaning against the instrument panel above the steering wheel.

I let him pull around me and back onto the highway before I started the engine. Well, that could have been a clusterfuck. I looked to the sky and gave a whispered prayer of thanks. I hadn't been sure anyone was listening for a long time now, but it was worth acknowledging providence when it was granted.

I drove a few more miles before pulling off into the brush past the welcome sign for the next small town. It was a chilly night in Roscoe, Texas—the temperature gauge on my dash said it was just a handful of degrees above freezing. No clouds, so it sure wasn't gonna snow. Nice enough for me. I'd had enough of humanity for the day.

And this was a perfect place to get rid of the drives from the vampire motel.

I pulled them from my pack and squeezed until their housings opened, throwing bits and pieces as far as I could in all directions. It left me with a little reel of black tape, which I burned on the shoulder of the empty highway. Once it burned and melted to use-lessness, I kicked at the ashes and bits with my boot, until it blended in with the dirt and gravel and other detritus along the side of the highway.

That done, I grabbed the blanket from behind the seats in the truck, locked the doors, and laid down in the bed. My breath created little puffs of cloud above my face as I watched the stars move across the sky. I crossed my arms behind my head as the chirping of crickets and movement of small noc-turnal animals in the vicinity lulled me to peaceful sleep.

ELEVEN

BEARS ARE NOT MIGRATORY CREATURES. They hole up and settle down and make dens. They may range out to follow their food, but otherwise stay in one place. So, when it became clear to me I could not put down roots, else the church would learn of my continued ability to draw breath when they otherwise thought me dead, I resigned myself to blending in with the common folk.

In the early days, before I had really figured things out, I had tried to settle down somewhere out of the way. A small village off the beaten path where I thought I could lay low. But I was learned in the ways of the Catholic church, and when people asked, I openly shared that information. Before long, I was having communal dinners with the villagers on Sundays, talking about God and Jesus and the original pillars of Christianity. I had never meant to minister to the people—I simply wanted them to have the information I was privy to, the information and wisdom Peter had dispensed as he was building the church.

Soon after my weekly meals had become regular occurrences, members of the church appeared and started asking questions. I should have known it was information that was no longer made public. The church had all but forgotten the days when Peter walked the Earth, and I was filling in the holes from stories told at services. The church expected the laity to take it on faith that the stories supported the lessons they preached, and though they very nearly did, there were details that had gotten left out.

Still, if the church was poking around among the people from my dinners, it would only be a matter of time before they found me.

So I disappeared.

I hid from the church and its werewolf packs. I hid from what was left of my fellow werebears. I largely ignored the purpose for my very existence unless I came into contact directly with a *consanguinea*. Even then, if they weren't in danger, I walked away. No need to interfere or draw attention unnecessarily.

But damn if my soul didn't sing when a *consanguinea* needed my help. And—much to my own chagrin—I offered it to them freely, asking nothing in return. I could not help myself.

I still did what I could to quell vampire uprisings as I came across them. Though even they had learned to keep their movements subtle and out of the eye of the common folk. The Crusades had been largely about them, or at least thanks to them, so they kept their heads down.

I let myself get lost among people and cultures. From medieval Europe and the heights of the Ottoman Empire to the Italian Renaissance and the early Holy Roman Empire, I saw civilizations rise and fall, though I stayed at the fringes of society and flowed with the winds. I used my jewelry-making to keep myself fed and clothed and busy, adapting new techniques and technologies into my repertoire as necessary, though I still vastly preferred the old ways.

I certainly didn't dare try to let myself fall in love.

I'd only have to watch that love grow old and die. And children were decidedly out of the question for me. My former werebear brethren had tried to procreate. The church had even encouraged it. But their women would not conceive. I suspect it was better that way. I could barely imagine what would come of a child born of a werebear and a human.

So, when women—or men, I wasn't picky—tried to love me, tried to keep me around, I left. Usually to the sound of their tears or shouted anger.

And I hated it.

I was envious of the humans who got to love and have families and die when their time came. Envious of creatures who lived their lives knowing there was a finality to it. Envious of those who could choose their paths with reckless abandon. Hell, I was even envious of those who were born into lives of servitude. At least they belonged in their world.

Somewhere along the way I stopped noticing the years passing.

They didn't matter.

I didn't matter.

It was a time marked by a lot of drinking in strange taverns and establishments, a lot of fighting in the shadows, a lot of fucking whoever was willing and interested, and a whole hell of a lot of feeling sorry for myself.

But then, people started to voyage across the sea. Spain and France sent settlers and established little towns and cities along the coast of what would later be America. The English even joined them. When I heard of these new colonies, I was certain it was a ticket to a new life for me. A do-over of sorts. Maybe there, the church didn't hold as much sway. Maybe there, I could finally be free of my past.

I should have known better even then.

TWELVE

I HAD WOKEN with the morning sun and started back on my journey, though my tail light detour had taken me two towns over out of the way. I'd lost half the day to ensure I didn't have a repeat of last night's bullshit with Officer Jimmy.

Worse, the drive through the tail end of Texas and the northeast corner of New Mexico was some of the most boring, nothing-going-on driving I had done this whole trip. The highway hypnosis had slammed into me like a freight train, and I'd had to stop somewhere in New Mexico before continuing on, but eventually I had crossed the Colorado state line.

This stupid expend-energy-in-bursts biology of mine was ridiculously inconvenient.

It was well after full dark when I had to stop an hour short of Colorado Springs. I wanted to push through, to keep going. But the truck needed fuel, and I was likely to cause an accident if I didn't get off the highway to break the monotony for a bit.

I stopped at a gas station and went inside to grab a coffee. The attendant had a little TV on the counter next to him.

He gave me a toothy grin as he rang me up.

Which is to say that he was missing a number of teeth haphazardly around his mouth. "You lookin' to do some elk huntin' on your way through?"

I shook my head. "Nah, not really my thing."

Well, it was, but I had more important things to worry about now.

"Alright then," he drawled. "Be careful if'n yuh change yer mind or yuh decide to go campin'. Trail cams're catchin' huge bears or sum'n out there."

I raised my eyebrow at him. "Oh yeah?"

Stupid young pups were getting themselves caught on camera all over.

He nodded as he handed me the change for my coffee. "They say you gotta treat 'em like a predator. Keep yer food in containers, don't run, an' make y'-self all big 'n' loud if they get in yer face."

I tipped my coffee at him. "Good advice. Thanks."

"Sure thing, mister," he said. "Drive safe."

I stepped into the cool night and stopped dead in my tracks.

Three vampires were leaning on my truck, and the stench of more hung thickly in the crisp air.

Fuck.

And odds were good I wasn't gonna get to leave here without taking them down.

I sighed.

"Big things moving across the country make waves," the sultry vampire who was all legs said as she pushed off my truck with her hip. "Our First doesn't like it when things make waves in his di-rection."

She ran her fingers across my chest as she tried to circle around behind me. I grabbed her wrist, halting her progress. Her eyes went wide.

First? There was a coterie with a First at its head this close to the *purgatum*?

Shit.

I crushed her wrist and threw her at the second vampire as he tried to circle around me.

The third vampire flew at me as the other two recovered, but it wasn't even a fight, really. He went down with a quick snap of the neck.

The first two, now recovered, threw themselves at me from opposite directions. I caught them and bashed their skulls against each other, turning them to sludge. No telling which bit of sludge belonged to which vamp, really.

As a few more vampires swarmed at me from behind my truck, it became clear that none of this coterie was a challenge. They were chaff, throwing their lives away against something decidedly outside their weight class.

It wasn't the church I had to worry about protecting the *purgatum* from.

It was fucking vampire royalty.

Another vamp down, her body thrown into the two beside me.

If the First out this way learned of her, her whole pack would be wiped out in the fight.

Fuck.

I snapped the neck of yet another bloodsucker before throwing the one at my back over my shoulder into the face of the one advancing on me.

Then a familiar scent came wafting in on the breeze. A scent I hadn't smelled in centuries.

Sandalwood and cloves.

I filled my lungs with it as a chill ran down my spine. That scent belonged to someone I had thought died along with my purpose in Bulgaria.

There was no way he was still alive.

Wild and reckless frenzy overcame me. I smashed the face in of the one in front of me and destroyed the three that had come around from behind the convenience store with swift efficiency as two more rushed in from the treeline.

The gas station attendant came out at some point, waving a shotgun. It went off once, uselessly, before another one of the bloodsuckers from the trees tore out his throat.

And then there were only two vampires left. Like the last pair at the motel, these, too, ran from me.

One of the remaining vamps looked over their shoulder as they dashed for the woods behind the gas station and shouted in a panicked voice, "What the hell is he?!"

A familiar figure stepped out from the trees, and my breath caught as a thrill of foreboding resonance ran through me. It stilled my wild frenzy.

Zacchaeus.

"More powerful than any gave him credit for," he said, meeting my gaze with a composed and somehow chilly curiosity.

Another wave of ice snaked down my spine at the sight of him, and I swallowed thickly.

His skin and hair were as pale as alabaster, and he had a light dusting of white scruff along his chin. He wore a white thermal shirt with khaki cargo pants, and his hands were jammed into his pockets. He strode with the same casual elegance I had always known him to possess. His pale eyes traced over me, studying me as he moved closer, his expression unreadable.

My heart lurched and kicked into overtime as the familiar dark chord thrummed in my muscles. I never thought a part of me would actually be relieved to see him alive. But we were not lovers anymore—we weren't even friends. I had tried to kill him, and the guilt of that had been a weight I had been carrying for centuries.

The resonance turned to ice that crackled and sent shards tinkling along my spine.

Zacchaeus was the First this close to the *purgatum*. God truly did have a twisted sense of humor—or perhaps irony. I could no sooner kill him than I could kill myself.

The *purgatum* was doomed.

And then something low and dark and deep sang through my veins, thrumming like the lowest notes from a bass guitar. A counter melody of sorts to the ominous song flowing through me in Zacchaeus' presence.

I couldn't let that happen.

I couldn't let Zacchaeus kill her.

And, God help me, I didn't know how I could possibly stop him once he knew of her existence.

I swallowed around a lump in my throat, trying to find my voice again as I looked away from the vampire's pale gaze. "Just leave, Zacchaeus. Walk away and—"

There was a flash of light—purple, green, and orange swirling and then coalescing into a warm daytime sky.

What the hell… ?

A couple of voices yelled in the distance behind Zacchaeus. The vampires who'd run, I thought— likely their death knells in the sudden sunlight. But their voices were soon drowned out by the chaotic sounds of battle.

This wasn't Colorado. The air smelled wrong, and the trees were gone.

We stood on a grassy plain of gently rolling hills. Great scaled lizards with musculature like a greyhound dog and giant leathery wings dotted the landscape. Those on the ground moved like great cats, their wings folded against their sides. They were taller than the armored soldiers around them, even the ones on horseback. Those in the sky had wingspans easily three or four times larger than they were nose-to-tail and flew more gracefully than anything that size had any business doing. Many fought with each other. Some had glowing runes and sigils carved into their scales. All of them were angry.

Were those dragons?! What the fuck?!

On a nearby hill, a creature shaped like the other dragons, but much larger, seemed to be comprised of the very shadows themselves. Malevolence roiled off the shadowy creature like a heat wave. It swiped a talon the size of a small farmhouse at a group of heavily armored knights carrying glowing golden blades, and they flew back into their compatriots.

Holy shit.

Nearby, a group of men and women in long robes waved their arms and staves, casting spells with blue and red-orange effects swirling to attack and deflect those from others. Some of the robed figures faced off against other armored and armed soldiers on horseback. Lightning shot down in fits and spurts all over the battlefield from clouds that held no hint of a storm. Smoldering balls of fire as big as a horse rolled around the battlefield and towering windstorms swept soldiers and rocks and boulders along in their wake. Inky shadows darted and danced among the soldiers, sowing death and chaos everywhere they went.

Zacchaeus spun in a circle as I had, taking it all in with an air of absolute confused bewilderment.

And I was just as bewildered.

He backed up until his shoulder brushed against mine, sending a shimmer of dark notes through me. As the battle pressed closer, his back flattened against me and the song in my veins grew louder. I closed my eyes to its strange, yet familiar, comfort. The *only* thing that was familiar in this wild fantasy scape.

Not now. I shook my head.

Wherever we were, whatever had happened, I certainly didn't have time to enjoy a moment of reminiscence with a creature that I had tried to kill. Not with a full battle worthy of any epic fantasy tale raging all around us.

"This is a neat trick," I called to him, hoping he could hear me over the sounds of the battle. "But it'd be better if you'd done it the other way around!"

"Day to night?" He shrugged against my shoulders. He was taller than me by a few inches. "Perhaps. But this isn't me. I thought you might have learned this illusion somewhere."

I rumbled out a laugh as I gestured to the dragons and the impossible creatures made entirely of water and fire trundling along the battlefield. "This is no illusion, and no magic I know can create such things."

The battle had pressed upon us now, and soldiers in black armor had almost surrounded us, their blades carved with glowing purple runes that smoked green. They fought soldiers with shining armor and weapons carved with glowing golden runes.

Fuck. I didn't want to know what happened if either of us got hit with one of those runed weapons.

I pulled Zacchaeus away from the wild swing from one of the soldiers in black, and he returned the favor as the spear of a shining soldier brushed a hair's breadth away from me.

As we recovered, there was another flash of swirling purple, orange, and green light, and we were back at the edge of the gas station lot, stumbling over the curb where the asphalt met the grass. The chill of November in Colorado slammed into me, and I took a breath to try to slow the pounding of my heart.

Zacchaeus' elbow was still hooked in mine. The song of him flowed through me as it ever had.

I swallowed thickly again, unhooking my elbow as I sidled away from him. "Not my circus."

He closed the distance between us again with smooth grace. "Not my monkeys."

The barest hint of a smile pulled at his lips. He smoothly raised his hand to my face and brushed my cheek with the same tenderness he had done ages ago, sending another shining melody through me. Tears shone in his pale eyes.

I hadn't known vampires were even capable of crying.

"It is good to see you again," he murmured.

Tension flowed from my shoulders and I blew out a breath as I leaned into his hand, reveling in the song flowing into me, tight and resonant as a plucked harp string.

Maybe there was time for a moment here.

But then his grip hardened.

He tore his hand from my face, his nails raking along my skin as the music abruptly halted. The absence of his touch left a single note of a minor chord ringing in me, like a piano key absentmindedly tapped, and warmth trickled from the places his nails scraped.

"I thought you died in Bulgaria." His voice was a whisper, but it held the pain of centuries.

He turned away then, and a whisper of wind cloaked him in a shadow that tore him from my sight as if he'd never been there.

I wiped the blood from my cheek and looked at my reddened fingertips. It had been a long time since anything had left me wounded.

To the nothingness where he'd been, I replied, "I spent too long wishing I had."

THIRTEEN

FATHER LUCIUS HAD LONG BEEN the one in charge of providing assignments to me and my werebear brethren. So, when he called me into his sparse office that spring evening, I answered his call without hesitation. It had been just over one hundred and fifty years since I'd killed Longinus, and my status within the church had been greatly elevated as a result of my victory over the vampire.

As I entered the office, a resonance filled me. It was like holy light had spilled directly into my veins. It rang in my ears and thrummed through my muscles like a plucked harp string.

Sitting on a stool next to the fireplace was a pale, skinny child—a little boy, barely as tall as my thigh.

"Ah, Kristos," Father Lucius said warmly. "Come in, come in."

He poured me a cup of wine and gestured to the child as he handed it to me.

"Kristos, this is Zacchaeus. He is—"

"*Consanguinea*," I breathed, falling to my knees near the boy. I had never met one of the line of Mary before. But I was as sure of it as I was the sun would rise in the morning and the moon at night.

Father Lucius smiled. "Yes. He is *consanguinea*. His family has brought him here to us. They say the poor dear cannot be out in the sunlight, else his skin burns and he vomits aught he has eaten."

I looked to the child as my mouth fell slack and my brow furrowed in pity. An ache settled in my chest, a sour note clanging against the holy light in my veins. This poor boy could not revel in the beauty of the days the Lord granted us?

"His family cannot afford to feed a child who cannot eventually help them work their land," Father Lucius continued. "And as he is *consanguinea*, I am sure I do not have to impress upon you his value to us."

"Not at all, Father," I replied. "What do you ask of me?"

I studied the pale child. He was so small. The ache in my chest deepened for his family's need to free themselves of him.

"I need you to guard him, Kristos. Help ensure he gets to his lessons safely. You must be the shadow he can stand in—the shadow he can grow in."

I nodded and placed my cup on the floor as I reached a hand out to the boy. He looked up at me. Bless him, even kneeling I was taller than him. His pale eyes seemed almost silver in the candlelight of Father Lucius' office.

Slowly, tentatively, the boy placed his hand in mine as he stood. The holy light that had spread through me upon entering the office seemed to dance along my skin at his touch. My heart filled nearly to bursting with the need to protect this child—this *consanguinea*—and my vision blurred as I gently curled my fingers around his.

Until that moment, I had thought my purpose had been killing vampires. Their deaths sang little chords of light through me as I ended them. But when faced with a tiny, fragile *consanguinea* child, I realized the truth—Peter had created us to protect the legacy of Jesus of Nazareth. The light flowing through me sang the undeniable truth of it.

"Greetings, Zacchaeus," I said to him in as gentle a tone as I could manage, my voice a little hoarse. "I am Kristos of Athens."

He studied my hand for a long moment. I swallowed around the gravel in my throat, wondering if he could feel the resonant music too.

Then he looked up at me again. "Greetings." His voice was too solemn for a child so small.

With my other hand, I pulled the wooden cross on a leather cord free from my shirt, and pulled it over my head. Releasing his hand, I placed the necklace around his neck.

"I am going to take care of you, okay?"

He nodded.

"Father Lucius, please bear witness." I looked up and nodded once to the Father before returning my attention to Zacchaeus, whose wide, silvery eyes continued to study me. "So long as I draw breath, Zacchaeus, nothing on this Earth will ever harm you."

"A bold oath, brother Kristos," Father Lucius said, his face slack. "A bold oath, indeed." The latter seemed to be more to himself than to either of us.

But he looked like he had more to say about it. The boy examined the cross I had given him, turning it over in his hand as I waited for Father Lucius to continue.

"It is one I intend to keep," I replied finally, when he didn't elaborate. I met the gaze of the small, pale boy in front of me and nodded once. "This is what I was created to do."

FOURTEEN

THERE ARE MOMENTS, entire days sometimes, whose importance demands they be remembered in exacting detail. Moments or days whose gravity insists they be etched onto your soul. Perhaps they are days you'd give anything to do over. Or moments you wish would never end. Or days whose very existence changed everything you thought you knew about the world.

Zacchaeus had flourished under the church's tutelage, growing into a quick-witted and wise young man. The skinny, too-small child grew to be taller than I, though considerably less bulky. Where I was broad, dark muscles, Zacchaeus was slim, pale elegance. He had started as a simple acolyte and errand boy—lighting candles, gathering supplies, relaying missives from one father to another. His graceful hands produced beautiful writing, and the leadership often asked him to transcribe their lengthy meetings. As he grew, he traveled to neighboring towns for supplies and correspondence, venturing farther and farther from the church the older he got.

And I was his faithful shadow.

I sat outside the church meetings, working on

jewelry to stay busy while I waited for my charge, often gifting pieces to him. I loomed in the shadows during his recreation with the other acolytes, a steady reminder that Zacchaeus was not to be trifled with. I traveled with him anywhere he went, both within the church grounds and without.

It was a safe assignment, to be his guardian, but it was one I took great pride in. And, at Father Lucius' request, not once did I tell him what I was. Nor did I tell him of the evils that roamed the night, the evils my brethren hunted. My charge simply thought me a very capable warrior of the church. It was true enough.

Zacchaeus marked his nineteenth year on the day his life—and mine—changed forever.

The day progressed with as much normality as any other day within the church. Zacchaeus broke his fast and then sat in morning prayer for a time before attending meetings. I sat in the hall outside, finishing my work on a brooch of pearls and yellow gemstones in a starburst pattern set in gold. I wrapped the settings with a fine gold wire before holding it up to the light from the window at the end of the hall. The meeting adjourned, and clergymen filed out of the room with stacks of papers and books. Zacchaeus emerged as I pushed a few errant loops of wire into shape.

It had been some time since I'd last gifted him one of my creations, and I pinned it to his tunic as he drew close.

"Another year older," I said to him with a smile. "And hopefully another year wiser."

Zacchaeus examined the brooch and beamed at me. "Thank you, Kristos! It is like a sun pinned to my breast."

We had lunch in the common room amongst the clergy and my brethren, exchanging pleasantries about the day and season. We spent the afternoon in the garden, under the heavy shade of fig and olive trees. There was a cool breeze, and it was a welcome relief from the almost oppressive warmth within the rooms of the cathedral this time of year.

During the evening meal, a runner came with the message that the church's much-delayed incense order was finally ready. By that time, night had fallen. Zacchaeus offered to go, and since it was a simple errand within the city, there was no reason not to let him.

None of us could have known. Or at least, that's what I tell myself. And I cannot be sure whether it was arrogance or complacence that drove my folly that evening.

We were more than 150 cubits past the gates when I smelled the rotten decay of vampires.

There hadn't been any vampire incursions in the city from what I'd seen or smelled while on errands with Zacchaeus, so I assumed there could not possibly be too many for me to protect my charge from. Still, better to get him to safety if I didn't want him to learn what the church was not ready to explain to him.

"Get back behind the gates, Zacchaeus." I kept my voice low but forceful as I scanned the area for the bloodsuckers.

I was not prepared for twenty or more of the earthbound demons to pounce on us, pouring out of alleyways on either side of the path and cutting us off from the gates.

My charge had not moved.

I glanced at Zacchaeus. His pale eyes were wide with shock at the bloodsuckers' speed.

And the vampires were too close for him to beat them to the gates now.

With a growl deep in my chest, I shoved him

roughly behind me and launched myself at the closest vampires, breaking their necks with a quick grip-and-flick motion.

From there, the fight blurred. I fought the vampires in droves, counting as best I could for the report I would inevitably have to give to Father Lucius. But in my frenzy to kill the vile creatures, I lost sight of Zacchaeus.

I thought it had been only twenty. But there was scrabbling and fighting behind me even as I pulled what should have been the last vampires from me. I spun around with a frustrated growl.

Zacchaeus struggled futilely against the grasp of two more of them. I hadn't kept as good a count as I thought I had. The jaws of one were sunk savagely into his shoulder, while the other scrabbled and slurped at his forearm.

Zacchaeus may have been *consanguinea*, but he was still only human.

He was facing the church gates. He'd had enough forethought to attempt to reach sacred ground. Perhaps he had listened at the doors of my own meetings with my brethren. Or, most likely, he was just fleeing the direction I had shoved him. It didn't matter which anymore.

I effortlessly tore the heads from the vampires attacking him.

Zacchaeus' pained scream as I pulled their jaws from his body is one I'll never clear from my head. The skin on his forearm was ragged, matching the sickeningly wide wound where his neck met his shoulder. There was too much blood, and his heartbeat had already begun to slow, the beautiful resonance between us fading.

I didn't call for help. I couldn't. I had made a solemn vow to protect a scrawny little boy nearly fifteen years prior.

And I had failed him.

The bile of my shame stuck in my throat, silencing me as I held the head and shoulders of the pale young man in my lap. His silvery eyes were nearly purple in the night. He reached a hand for my face and I took it in my own, pressing his palm to my cheek as tears dripped onto his forehead.

I didn't even have words to comfort him. The shame and grief tore them from my mind.

Zacchaeus' heart beat its last and his hand went limp. I choked on a sob as the fading chord between us went silent. I brushed his nearly-white hair from the pale skin of his forehead and placed a gentle kiss in the spot I had cleared.

The world blurred to incoherence. There were no words for my failure. It was all I could do to blindly gather him into my arms and haul myself to my feet.

FIFTEEN

THE ACRID SCENT of scorched flesh filled the air, cutting through the rotten stink of vampires and the metal of spilled blood. Something sharp bit into my shoulder. A rush of euphoria flowed through me as the resonance I had known moments before returned in a somewhat darker key. I blinked to clear my vision and saw Zacchaeus' white eyelashes flutter closed as he slurped at the meat of my shoulder.

The cross I had given him years ago was now burning his skin.

The damned bloodsuckers turned him!

Those God-forsaken earthbound demons had enough control to decide whether to drink from him or to turn him, and they *chose* to turn him.

And on the heels of that realization, came the knowledge that I couldn't do the one thing I knew I was supposed to. God forgive me, I couldn't kill him.

So I dropped his legs and struck my fist into the back of his skull, knocking him out.

His wounds closed. The one in my shoulder didn't.

I didn't have time to wonder at it. I tore the cross from his neck, snapping the leather cord, and jammed it into the pouch at my waist. I had to get away from the church gates. With a shaky breath, I pressed my free hand to my face and racked my brain.

There was a bathhouse on the south side of town —the seedier part of town.

Perfect.

I didn't even look over my shoulder to learn who might already have borne witness to Zacchaeus' death and subsequent not-death. I didn't dare. I had to pray none had. If only I could be so lucky.

I rushed to the bathhouse. A young boy opened the door at my insistent pounding.

"I am sorry, sir," the boy said, eying my bloodied tunic and injured charge. "The bathhouse is closed for the evening."

"I understand, of course." I shifted Zacchaeus' weight in my arms and pried the brooch from his tunic. The one I had gifted him earlier that day. I sucked on my lip and offered it to the boy in an outstretched palm. "But perhaps your master will accept this to allow us a quiet place for a handful of hours."

The little boy's dark eyes widened as the gems in the brooch caught the light. "A moment, sir."

With a hurried click, he shut the door, and his scampering footsteps slapped along the tile away from the entrance. Moments later, the slapping of small feet was replaced with the heavier steps of someone larger. The door creaked open.

"We are closed, sir," the manager said, his eyebrow arched at me, but he swung the door wide to allow me and my charge entry.

I breathed a sigh of relief as I stepped off the street. He quietly closed the door behind us.

"My thanks, sir," I said, offering him the brooch.

He nodded as he took it. "I'll not ask what's happened to you and the man you carry, and I have no bandages to offer you. You must be gone before dawn."

I adjusted Zacchaeus' weight once again. "Your generosity is greatly appreciated."

The boy returned, two oil lamps in hand. He handed one to me before stepping back behind the manager.

I took Zacchaeus into the dressing chamber and laid him on a bench. His heart beat faintly, likely from the blood he'd managed to drink from me. I sat on a bench halfway across the room from him, facing him, and waited for him to wake.

He didn't smell like the vampires I was used to. Not yet, at least. He still smelled of the oils he'd used when he last bathed, though there was an underpinning of sweat to his scent.

My shoulder throbbed with a sharp but small ache. A reminder that he had bitten me.

It still hadn't healed.

I craned my neck to examine what precisely he'd done to my shoulder, but I couldn't get a good angle to see anything beyond the fact that it was still oozing blood. I touched the wound with my fingers, gently feeling along the edges of ragged skin.

I'd been bitten by vampires before—bitten, clawed, sliced with blades, pierced with arrows. All had healed. So why wasn't this?

The beating of his heart faded again and then stopped, cutting off my wonder, and my throat closed once more. I knew he would wake, but I had spent too long memorizing the beat of his heart, the rhythm of his breathing, to be at peace with the absence of either. Water lapped against the edges of the pools in the bathhouse, echoing the grief welling in me.

A moment later, Zacchaeus woke with a hissing

growl and sat up. The dark music humming between us brightened ever so slightly.

He squinted at me in the faint light of the lamp, but I knew he could see me as well as I could see him. Darkness was no longer a blinding factor for him.

"I have never heard the heartbeats of others," he said. "Only my own, or that of someone I held close to me."

I nodded gravely, raking a hand through my hair. "I know."

He closed his eyes. "But I can not hear mine."

I swallowed around another lump of shame. "That's because you don't have one anymore."

Zacchaeus shook his head. "That can't be true. I wouldn't still be breathing—wouldn't be sitting here —if my heart didn't beat."

I leaned forward, resting my elbows on my thighs. "Breathing isn't something you have to do anymore, either."

"What do you mean? Why can I hear your heart-beat, Kristos?" He stood from the bench and stepped closer to me, his voice growing thick and husky. "Why does the sound of it and the scent of the wound on your shoulder make my mouth water?"

I slapped a hand over where he'd bitten me as I averted my gaze and gritted my teeth. The church had sheltered him, and I was just as complicit in such sheltering. They had done him a disservice by disallowing me to discuss what I am and what I fight with him. But there was no reason not to tell him now.

"Because you are an earthbound demon, Zacchaeus. That's what attacked us outside the church gates. They tried to kill me, and they turned you. They must have had their eyes on you for a while now—watching, waiting. I didn't think there were any here in the city."

His voice was very quiet. "How can you be sure?"

I pulled the wooden cross from my pouch. "This cross is the one I gave to you the day I met you. It was carved from the wood used to crucify Jesus, making it a divine relic. As such, it is blessed beyond even the rosaries the bishops wear. You cannot touch it with bare skin lest you be burned by its power. It scorched against your chest after you fell."

Zacchaeus furrowed his brow and brushed fingers across his chest, but the wound had already healed. There was no burn to match what I'd told him. So he reached for the cross, his mouth agape. His canines were extended. The hair on the back of my neck prickled. As his fingers closed around the bit of wood, the scent of burning flesh filled the air again and I met his eyes.

"I have been hunting earthbound demons all of my very long life. I hunted them until the day the church asked me to guard you, a child of Mary, *consanguinea*."

He held my gaze for a long moment before releasing the cross, shaking his hand from the burn. "That makes you one of the bears, doesn't it?"

The quiet in his voice was like ice down my spine. I said nothing, and I did not look away as I palmed the cross. He had grown into a truly clever young man.

"I thought you might be. The priests danced around the subject in their meetings, but I'd taken notes for enough of them to piece it together. They don't want the laity to know about the bears and what they fight."

His head fell into his hands as he sat on the bench next to him. He blew out a breath and was quiet for a long moment.

"I'm what you fight, aren't I?" His voice was nearly silent.

"You are now," I confirmed.

He lifted his head, his mouth slack and his eyebrows raised. I hurried to sit beside him, wrapping my arm around his shoulder in familiar reassurance.

"But you are also *consanguinea*," I told him. "Which means my purpose is to protect you."

The resonance that had gained a darker tone became a more vibrant thrum through my muscles at the declaration.

"How can I be sure you aren't saying that to get closer to me? How can I be sure you won't kill me?" There was a quiet accusation in his whispered tone.

"I cannot kill you, Zacchaeus." The response was almost automatic, yet I was as sure of its truth as I was of my own name.

He looked at me then, his expression uncertain.

I took a deep breath and held up the cross, holding his gaze. "I swear to you, Zacchaeus, I will never lie to you. For as long as either of us shall live."

Zacchaeus turned his body and threw his arms around me, pressing the cross between my hand and the linen tunic covering his chest. I hesitated to return the embrace, but could not stop myself in the end. He was still my *consanguinea*.

I smirked against his hair. "Besides, I've had plenty of opportunity to kill you by now."

He stiffened, his fingers digging into my back with little pinpricks.

I shook my head. "I am unconcerned with a lone vampire. More than twenty ambushed us. They're all dead. If I was going to kill you, you would already be gone."

He relaxed at that.

"What will you do?" His breath was warm against me. His tongue lapped against the wound on my shoulder, and the euphoria spread through me again. I closed my eyes as it washed over me.

"Stop that," I said sternly, my voice too thick.

I shouldn't like his mouth on me like that. I couldn't. He would drink me dry if I let him. I gripped the soft, nearly-white curls on the back of his head and pulled his face from me.

"It's sweet," he crooned. His hands moved away from me.

"It's my *blood*, Zacchaeus. It belongs inside of me." I furrowed my brow. "And it usually heals by now."

He shook his head and I released him, my thoughts still on my shoulder. Nothing in this world had left lasting wounds on me since I became a creature of the church. I sighed. I'd have to worry about that after I figured out what to do with him.

He looked at his hands. Sure enough, the tips of his fingers shone with blood from where he'd gripped me. With a furtive glance at me, he brought his hands to his mouth.

I turned my head away. I couldn't watch what he'd become.

"I can't take you back to the church," I told him, musing aloud. "Even if I wanted to, even if they would accept you as you are now, you are incapable of stepping foot on the grounds."

My voice thankfully covered the sound of him licking his fingers clean.

I thought for a moment. There was nowhere within the city he would be safe. And if anyone within the church saw the attack, they would know I did not immediately kill the earthbound demon my charge had become.

"I'm going to have to get you out of here. Away from the city, beyond the reach of the church."

"They will reject you for it, Kristos," Zacchaeus said. "You'll never be welcome among them again."

I nodded gravely, my heart a lead weight in my chest. "I know. But I cannot stand by and watch them kill you. And I certainly cannot do it myself." The thrum in my muscles became a warmth spreading throughout my body at the truth of it. How ironic that the purpose I was built for would have me protect the very creature the church had specifically intended for me to destroy.

SIXTEEN

I HAD friends in the city, beyond those connected with the church. There were merchants I had worked with. Merchants who kept an eye out for a specific brand of violence along their routes. Merchants whose families I had seen grow up.

One such family had been on their way out of town. I had not asked for details. I knew their trade route took them out of the country, away from the reach of the church. That was enough. They helped me slip Zacchaeus quietly away that night, my cross in the pouch at his belt. The chord between us had faded as their cart pulled away from the town, leaving a hollow silence in its place.

Alone, I returned to the church to face the judgment that almost certainly awaited me there.

It had been hours since the attack, the light of dawn had burned away the corpses of the fallen vampires, and no one stopped me as I returned to my bedchamber. If no one saw the fight, they may have surmised that Zacchaeus had been turned, that I had managed to kill him, and that his corpse had burned with the rest of the vampires.

If only I could be so lucky.

At least the wound in my shoulder had stopped oozing blood.

I lit a candle on my desk and wrapped my shoulder, ignoring the tiny wounds on my back, before changing into a clean tunic. I gathered a fresh candle from the drawer of my cabinet and the rolled leather containing my jeweler's tools. I could not help but stare at the latter.

My guilt ate at me.

Just hours prior, while the sun still shone, I had finished the brooch I gave him for his birthday. That same brooch had bought us a place to hide while I figured out what to do next. Just hours prior, Zacchaeus had been breathing because he needed to, not because it was habit. Just hours prior, I had failed to protect Zacchaeus from the one thing Peter had converted me to stop.

God forgive my failure.

My vision blurred with tears and I gulped down the lump in my throat. I roughly jammed a clean tunic into the sack and placed it under my desk.

Nothing left to do but wait.

Even if the church—if Father Lucius—could forgive me, I would still leave.

I had failed all of them, and it would be quite some time before I was ready to forgive myself for that… if ever.

I sat on my bed to wait, my hands folded in my lap.

I didn't have to wait long.

Less than an hour after my return, Father Lucius came to my door and I stood to answer it. He was with three of my brethren.

I knew Erastus well. He was practically a taller version of myself. He had been converted by the church the same year I had and we had been on a number of missions together. The other two, Akakios and Salathiel were younger than I, and I did not know them as well as I should have liked.

Three brethren alongside Father Lucius confirmed what I already knew.

This was the end of my time with the church.

Father Lucius' voice was pleading, but firm. "You must tell us where you have sent him, Kristos."

He meant Zacchaeus, of course.

The three bears—my brothers—placed themselves at strategic intervals around the room.

They expected a fight.

Father Lucius watched me with dark eyes, letting the silence stretch before huffing out a disappointed breath. "Attendants at the gates heard the fight. They saw what happened. We know he was turned. We know you did not kill him."

He stepped closer to me, placing a gentle hand on my shoulder. "I am not disappointed you could not kill him once he was turned. He grew up in your care. Even animals defend their young."

I turned my head and ran a hand over my face. The heartbeats of my brethren were strong and steady. Mine beat in a syncopated rhythm to theirs. It had matched before. I swallowed around the shame and grief.

He squeezed my shoulder. "But you know what must be done, Brother Kristos. Tell us where he has gone that we may relieve you of this burden."

"I cannot, Father." My voice was hoarse with heartache at the choice I knew had to be made. "I know not where he lies."

"The careful words of one who knows he can only speak truth to us," Salathiel said, resentment in his tone.

Father Lucius raised a hand, forestalling more commentary.

I met the golden eyes of the two bears in my field

of vision, since Erastus was behind me, over my left shoulder. Akakios studied me with curiosity, Salathiel with seething anger.

I don't think any of my brethren could have done differently than I had in the same situation. But I also don't think any of them could have known that.

My gaze shifted back to Father Lucius. "Vampire or no, he is still *consanguinea*. I cannot be party to his destruction."

Erastus hissed in frustration.

Father Lucius' expression fell, and his head drooped like a wilted flower. He swallowed thickly, took a deep, steadying breath, and looked to me once more. A hardness settled in his gaze.

"You know the choice you have made." There was no question to his tone, merely a detached evenness. "You are hereby excommunicated, Kristos of Athens. You are no longer welcome among the church and laity, and you are to leave immediately."

The words stabbed hot pokers into the void Zacchaeus' dark resonance had filled just hours ago. I sucked in a breath as Father Lucius turned sharply from me and snuffed the candle on my desk. Akakios and Salathiel flanked the door as Father Lucius stepped into the hallway beyond.

Erastus was still behind me. "You knew the church could not abide your choice. This is greater than you, Kristos—greater than any of us."

"We are to escort you off the grounds," Akakios said.

I nodded once and gathered the sack from under my table, slinging it over my shoulder.

The three werebears escorted me into the churchyard, where a small bag waited at the bottom of the last column before the wooden gates.

Erastus lifted the bag and handed it to me. "Provisions. That you don't starve." There was a hint of a smirk pulling at his mouth.

I blinked at the bag. Father Lucius and the others would have known I was unlikely to starve, I could hunt and even eat raw meat as a bear.

But there was not time to investigate the offering, so I nodded in thanks as I took the bag from him.

"You know the church is forgiving, Brother." His voice was barely above a whisper. "They will welcome you back if you bring proof of the boy's demise. Do not choose an earthbound demon's life over your own."

"He is still *consanguinea*, Erastus." My voice was firmer than I'd meant it to be.

Salathiel spun to face me. "He is corrupted!"

Erastus speared him with a look and then turned his face back to me as he placed a hand on either shoulder. "You know as well as I, there is no saving him now. I beg of you, Brother, do not choose this path."

"It is already done. I wish you and my brothers endless success on your future hunts."

He clenched his jaw and I turned from him. I met the eyes of Akakios and Salathiel once more in turn. "Stay safe, brothers."

Akakios swallowed audibly and nodded. Salathiel crossed his arms, his face a shuttered mask of anger, presumably at my choice.

"And you, Kristos," Erastus said behind me, his voice quiet. "The Lord bless and keep you."

I looked over my shoulder at him and nodded.

As I passed from the city that day, a quiet anger roiled through me. Anger at the vampires who had taken Zacchaeus from me. Anger at myself for not having the strength to deny my purpose. Anger at the Lord God himself who had allowed events to unfold in such a manner.

But most of all, I was angry that I could not be angry at Father Lucius.

He was human. His life was short. And what he wanted of me was perfectly within reason for him to expect. Denying him that left him no choice but to excommunicate me. Allowing me to stay would only have encouraged further insubordination from the bears, and—if pushed—the church could not stop us should we decide to eliminate them and take over. We wouldn't do such a thing, of course. Killing humans went against all we stood for. And we had honor, after all.

But the church still thought us creatures of free will. They could not understand what we had given up for the power to destroy the earthbound demons. Father Lucius didn't know I simply *could not* kill Zacchaeus—or any *consanguinea*, for that matter—even if I wanted to. Even if it meant my own life.

SEVENTEEN

I AM OVERLY cautious of attachment, as it only leads to trouble for a creature such as I. Unable to procreate, and long-lived enough to be effectively immortal, my only legacy would be in the extermination of vampires, and the safekeeping of *consanguinea*. I certainly should know better than to allow myself to love. But I had been wandering on the outskirts of the Holy Roman Empire for eighty years when I met her. The only woman I'd ever loved since the passing of my wife and children.

Aurelia.

She was a widow, originally from Dacia, a place history has all but forgotten thanks to its constant ravaging by the Germanic tribes of the time. She was also a weaver of household items: rugs, blankets, and curtains. Her patterns were beautifully intricate and wildly colored, and she had a sharp tongue for any who dared insult her wares.

Lord only knows what they expected from a blind weaver anyway.

But she had the most gorgeous branching scars that trailed down her back from her right shoulder. She had somehow managed to survive the lightning strike that took her vision without clouding her beautifully dark eyes. And she was probably the kindest soul I had ever met, despite her biting wit. She frequently fed street urchins and stray animals alike from her stew pot, and gave the children blankets to keep warm in the winter.

She even had kind words for an excommunicated bear—and a fair bit more than that—though she never pushed to learn anything about my past. She appreciated that I didn't feel the need to fill silences, and enjoyed the simple boon of having a man around in a society that saw her—a childless widow—as a burden.

And she truly came alive in the night. She was a generous yet demanding lover, with an appetite that was nigh upon insatiable. She filled the quiet hurts of the loss of Zacchaeus with her love, and she never once needed or asked for any explanation as to what I was.

I was in too deep when I realized I loved her as earnestly and completely as she loved me.

I tried to leave her, *wanted* to leave her, but could never bring myself to do so. I could not bear the thought of breaking her heart again when she had already lost so much. I was going to watch her grow old and die, and there was nothing I could do about it. She was going to figure out what I was, or at least ask far too many questions, as soon as she realized I was not growing wrinkled and fragile as she eventually would.

The church hadn't made any other bears since Peter's death ages before, and even if they had, they wouldn't dare convert a blind widowed weaver. Hell, the simple fact that she was a woman meant even Peter would have dismissed her out of hand.

But when the church moved on to creating werewolves, they had the forethought to include women.

After all, by then they had seen the bears' difficulty to procreate. Their existence was a well-kept secret, but wolves had even ventured out to the edges of the Roman Empire in their hunts for vampire nests, passing through Aurelia's village on their travels. I had scented the wild creatures for what they were, and gave them a wide berth in case they were keen to quarrel.

And I was positively consumed by the fear of losing her. I loved her more than I had words to describe, and my heart ached at the mere thought of her eventual death.

I was so very naive.

In time, I convinced Aurelia to travel to Rome, to the very church where I had been excommunicated. I had to try to convince them to convert her. If they would agree, I could finally tell her all of what I am, share with her all of me. The wolves had to be at least as long-lived as I was. Surely the church could grant her this boon. And I would do aught they asked of me if they would. Aught, that is, but kill Zacchaeus.

The wolves at the church gates were certainly less than eager to help me, but they eventually led me to a small chapel that had been traditionally used for small, family-centered services. There, they bid me wait for Father Quintus.

When the Father arrived, he paused a moment at the entryway, taking in my appearance. He had Brother Salathiel with him, and when pressed, he flatly refused my request.

"You have not completed the last order the church asked of you," Salathiel snarled. "You think the church would welcome one such as you back with open arms?"

Father Quintus placed a hand on Salathiel's shoulder, stopping him from adding further commentary. He looked at me solemnly. "An eye for an eye, Kristos."

I could not restrain my anger, but managed to keep my voice to a low rumble. "How ungodly of you."

Father Quintus tsked at me. "Judge not lest ye be judged, Kristos. You are excommunicated. We are but men, and though our lives are short, our memories are long. Bring us proof of the demise of the earthbound demon you failed to cull and perhaps we can revisit this conversation."

And with that, he left. Salathiel remained, watching me.

"Your absence has been felt among us, Kristos," he whispered. "We are not as numerous as we were in decades past. The church has grown reckless with our lives. With their new creations, we have become expendable."

I narrowed my eyes at him. "Why tell me this?"

"Because when you return—*if* you return—you will likely be the last. We hear our death knell in every howl of the wolves' hunts."

I did not ask how many had fallen. I feared the answer. With a heart heavy with the knowledge of my love's mortality, we returned to Aurelia's village.

EIGHTEEN

AURELIA'S little house stank of vampire and… somewhat else. I inhaled deeply, trying to identify the scent. Sandalwood and cloves. I put myself between her and the door, but when I pushed it open, a low, deep thrum settled along my muscles. The sunlight fell on pale hair and a stranger turned to face me.

Only it was no stranger.

It was Zacchaeus.

And the sunlight was not burning him.

How on Earth… ?

The world slanted sideways as the dark resonance between us returned.

The boyish features I had known in him had settled into a face that warred with both innocence and violence. His strong chin was set with a man's confidence, and he looked at me with heavily lidded silvery eyes that were tinted pink in the light of sunset. His pale lashes caught the dying light like raindrops. His creamy white hair was still barely a shade brighter than his smooth skin. It was longer than he'd kept it during his time with the church, and the unruly curls had been tamed into gentle waves and tied back, though a few errant strands framed his face. He was as lean and elegant as I remembered him—more so, truly.

"What squatter has taken residence in my home?" Aurelia's voice cut through my wonder at his presence.

"No squatter," I whispered, patting her hand where it rested in the crook of my elbow.

Zacchaeus smiled and rose. "Only a friend."

I had nearly forgotten he was taller than me, that he no longer fit in my shadow. The music between us grew ever so slightly brighter.

Aurelia went to work bringing her home back to living condition, and Zacchaeus and I went for a walk to the banks of the river.

"I cannot say I am displeased to see you again," I said.

Zacchaeus smiled at me without malice. "But you want to know why I'm here."

I stole glances at him as we walked. This was not the same boy that had left Rome eighty years prior. "Indeed."

We paused by a grove of olive trees and he opened his palm in a sunbeam, the light splashing across his pale skin. He pointedly studied it for a moment before gazing into the distance.

"I could not be in the sun as a child," he said finally. "It would make my skin blister."

I nodded. "It's why Father Lucius called me to be your shadow."

His gaze returned to me. "Do you know there is no other vampire that can walk in daylight?"

"I know your kind has a certain... allergy to it."

Zacchaeus laughed, his head bobbing in agreement. "You could say that. As it turns out, the very nature of my birth may be the reason I can. Or at least, that is what I suspect. The truth of it matters not. Vampires all across this land see me as veritable royalty." He closed his hand into a fist and brought it behind his back, joining his other hand. "I find it odd to be in a position of power after a life of sub-servience to the church."

"You dance around the point, Zacchaeus."

He smiled at me then, watching my face like he was relearning its features. "It is good to hear my name from your lips."

I didn't have a response for it, but something was charged in the air nonetheless.

He turned and watched the river. "I want to help you, Kristos. The church has turned its back on you, but I will not. Your assistance in my escape let me carve a true life for myself. Let me return the kind-ness. Let me turn your love, and save you from the suffering of watching her grow frail."

My heart surged at the thought of a full lifetime with Aurelia, but I tempered it with truth. "You offer to make her a monster."

He tsked at me then, much like Father Quintus had, and pressed long fingers to his chest. "Do you think so little of me?"

I looked away from him, shaking my head. "Not you, Zacchaeus."

"I am different?"

"You are," I insisted, my brow furrowed. "And you know it. You are *consanguinea*. Aurelia is not."

"I was turned of the First, Kristos. Do you know what that means?" He raised an elegant white eye-brow at me.

I shook my head once and waited for him to explain.

"It means that even if I couldn't walk in the day-light, I'd be half revered by those you call monsters anyway. The vampire who turned me, though dead now, was the first vampire turned of the first vampire turned by Longinus himself."

"The world's first vampire." We said it at the same time.

His white eyebrows shot up. "You know of him."

"I killed him."

"How interestingly tantalizing." He waved his hand. "Well, all the same. Firsts are apparently to be revered. Your killing of one caused an imbalance I was able to fill. I have not turned any myself since that day outside the church gates. If I turn your Aurelia, she will be a true power—equal to me."

I pressed my lips into a line. Something about the way he said 'equal' was wrong. There was a lie there, I was certain. But Zacchaeus had never lied to me when he was my charge.

"Equal to you?"

"Nearly so," he replied coolly. "She would be too young, too fresh to carry all the power I do, and she will likely not be able to walk in the day as I do. But I will ensure she is not slighted for her dissimilarity."

Hm. Not quite equal then. She would be reliant on his good graces. There *was* an undeniable power radiating from him, and he carried himself with a surety the boy acolyte had never had.

I had to admit it was good to see. "She deserves a better life than killing others for her own survival."

He gave me a wry smile. "That is not the way things are done amongst mine. Aught we drink from are willing, unless they be enemies, and there is no point to killing a freely given source of life."

I sighed. "It is good to hear you are not as monstrous as those who have come before you. All the same, she would be a monster, an earthbound demon."

Zacchaeus placed a hand on my shoulder, his slender fingers squeezing gently. "She would be no more a monster than you are, my dear werebear. And you can stay with her, teach her as you did me."

I looked away from him. I was not convinced this was a generous offer. She would die, her heart would cease beating just as Zacchaeus' had so many years ago. And though she would wake again after, just as he had, she would no longer be able to feel the sun warm her face.

He patted my shoulder. "What I offer is more life than she would have without, and you won't have to watch her grow frail, watch the life leave her bones."

I looked up at him, studying his elegant features as I considered his words.

His face lit with realization and he released my shoulder, holding a finger in the air. "She is blind, is she not?"

I nodded. "She was struck by lightning years ago."

Zacchaeus gave me a knowing smile. "Then she will likely heal whatever cost her sight."

Well that certainly changed things. She would be able to see her art again. But it would twist her.

Except… she was so kind that she could probably stand a little darkness.

Surely she would forgive my presumptuousness.

I watched the river for a long while before turning to him again. "I hope she will not be appalled at her creations when she finally sees them. I am rather fond of her wild color schemes."

Back at Aurelia's little house, Zacchaeus waited for the sun to dip below the horizon before turning the woman I loved. Her sight returned when she woke from her not-death and she saw me, truly saw me, for the first time since I'd met her so many months ago. I could not help but revel in the elation of giving her my blood and, as her heart beat again, we told her of the bears, the wolves, and the vampires. I could not bear to think of her as an earth-bound demon, and refused to call her such.

And her fingers running through my fur as I was finally able to show her my bear form made my heart soar.

That night, I made love to a vampire for the first time in my life. I did not have to be gentle with her, did not have to fear breaking her. And she now had the stamina to keep up with me. We barely got a wink of sleep. It was freeing, and though her heart would beat and fade with each feeding, my own beat more fiercely with love for her then. For who I could be with her. For the possibilities before us.

NINETEEN

DESPITE NEARLY 400 years of life experience, I was so very naive to think Aurelia could still want me after being turned. Though, for a while, she did.

We left the Roman Empire together along with Zacchaeus, crossing the Danube and venturing into the land that would become Bulgaria. There, he had settled in a manor which had been long since abandoned and shuttered. Indeed, nearly half the town was seemingly abandoned buildings.

Only they were not so much abandoned as they were held by vampires who had no need or want of the daylight. The rest of the town was inhabited by their human livestock.

There, I quickly learned the difference between a human being kept as a feeder and their family. The former had the acrid death scent of vampire overlaying the otherwise bland sweat smell of human, while the latter smelled only vaguely of the earthbound demons feeding on their family.

As I lived alongside the daily ebb and flow of this vampire town, I found myself a frequent advisor to Zacchaeus. It was impossible not to be impressed with his keen mind and smooth confidence. The long hours he'd spent in meetings as an acolyte of the church had taught him that running an entire town —even one where the humans themselves were well-tended livestock—was not so different from running a church.

But Aurelia's affections had waned for a valiant creature such as I. In time, she had fallen for the one who changed her. She did not deny it when I confronted her about it in the hour just after dawn late that summer.

"It should come as no surprise to you, Kristos," she said, pulling a nightgown over her dark curls to cover the branching scar along with the rest of her beautiful body. "You as good as gave me to him when you bade him turn me."

"I did not ask him to."

"Perhaps not." She pulled her hair out from under the collar and pointed a finger at me. "But you did not refuse him. And I could no sooner refuse him now than I could go back to the life I've left behind."

"It was for you, Aurelia." My voice was thick with pain. "I could not bear to watch you grow old and frail."

"So it was selfishness that drove you. I thought better of you than that."

I shook my head and turned from her. "Perhaps it was. When he let it be known it could restore your sight, I-"

"You thought to take fate into your own hands." She put a hand on my shoulder, turning me to face her again. When I did, she placed a hand on my cheek. "I loved you, Kristos."

Loved.

Not love.

Loved.

The bottom dropped out of my stomach.

She continued as if the world had not ceased moving. "You are so noble and strong, how could I not? But what I am now is as different as night and day from the girl you met in the market."

"I love you, Aurelia." I could not help the desperation in my voice.

"In your own way, I am sure that is true. But how many others have you loved in your lifetime, Kristos?" With a sigh, she turned from me. "I am no fool. Had my life ended when it was meant to, you would have moved on and, eventually, fallen in love again."

"You are the first woman since the death of my family. The first since I became what I am. The first in nearly four hundred years."

"That only proves my point. I shall not be the last." She put a fist on her hip as she narrowed her dark eyes at me, an expression crossing her face that I had not seen in her before this moment: disdain. "Do you think you were the first broken thing I had mended by inviting you to my bed?"

I wish she had slapped me. "I… never gave a thought to it."

The smile that twisted her face was dark, devilish. "Of course not. Well, no matter. I will not take you to my bed again unless it is to break you, dear Kristos."

I took a breath and steeled myself, refusing to give her the satisfaction of my pain on display. I should have known better than to think turning her would not change her. I should have foreseen what she would become.

Becoming an earthbound demon always twists the nature of the human underneath.

My hands closed into tight fists and I turned away from her. Outside her doorway, I turned my chin over my shoulder. "You will never get the satisfaction, Aurelia."

Her voice carried into the hallway. "We shall see."

I would have left that day—I *should* have left that day. Were it not for Zacchaeus' earnest plea that I stay, I might have even succeeded.

"If you did truly kill the first of us," he said, sitting next to me, "then I would be deeply honored if you would resume your former position with me."

"You wish me to be your guardian once again?" I raised an eyebrow at him over my twelfth cup of wine.

"Coteries are not peaceful places, Kristos," Zacchaeus said before leaning close to me, his sandalwood and cloves scent filling my nose. He gently brushed hair from my ear, sending a thrill of song through me, and his voice grew low and husky. "And I would be lying if I told you guardianship was aught I desired of you."

I pulled away from him then, studying his face. Arousal threaded through his scent, but he spoke true. And, despite the wine in my system, my body reacted to him. It was not entirely unpleasant.

Holding my gaze, he brought my cup of wine to his lips and took a slow sip. I watched his throat bob as he swallowed my wine, and the resonance between us swirled into a darkly alluring chord. He brushed an errant drop of wine from his lip with the pad of his thumb.

I had never thirsted for a drop of wine as I had that particular drop.

Despite my years, I was so very naive. But the elegantly confident man before me bore so little resemblance to the unsure boy who grew up in my shadow that I thought nothing of it when his mouth crashed against mine, tasting of wine and inevitability.

In fact, I thought nothing of it when he took my shaft into his mouth, swirling his tongue around me with practiced ease as he guided me deep into his throat. Nothing of it to close my hand around his own pale erection, pumping until his seed spurted across my dark knuckles.

Nothing of it to bury myself inside him with reckless abandon day after day while my former lover slept.

And the harmony between us sang in my veins, dark and thick with elation.

I let it become habit, knowing that while he was mine in the daylight, he was hers when night fell. I let him drink from me, reveling in the euphoria that chased through me as the resonance between us brightened until his heartbeat faded once again, singing a dark chord into the music.

On the equinox that marked the last day before the harvest, I finally asked him if he felt the song between us as well.

He smiled at me, his pale skin naked and cool against the dark warmth of my side. "All this time and you never knew?" His mouth closed against mine, sending another thrum through me. "It is how I know we belong together." He wrapped an alabaster leg around my knee, spreading my legs wide as he wrapped long fingers around my shaft.

I rolled my hips against his grip, my eyes closing with pleasure as the melody sounded another dark note.

"Just like that," he whispered, his cool breath against my neck sending goose pimples along my skin.

Pinpricks followed his breath and the euphoria flowed through me as his hand pumped along my length in time with the resumed beating of his heart. The song we shared built to a nearly frenzied crescendo before crashing with a beautifully full chord as my seed spilled across his knuckles. Pulling his lips from my throat as my ecstasy subsided, he licked his fingers clean.

"No wonder he always smells of you." Aurelia's voice cut my joy short.

Zacchaeus was unfazed by the intrusion and leaned closer to me, his voice so soft I could barely hear it over his heartbeat. "That note is always my favorite." His tongue caressed the outer edge of my ear and a wave of heat followed the dark note singing in my veins.

Aurelia dropped her robe. She was naked beneath it. "Certainly you can find room for another amongst your blankets?"

"No." My voice was firm, but my body betrayed me.

"Hmm," Zacchaeus mused, drinking in the sight of her body. "Of course there's room for you. Just mind your former lover there, my dear. He is prickly."

She was all hips as she moved to the bed and crawled over top of me, meeting my eyes in challenge. "I'm sure he can forgive things said in anger."

Loved.

I would not. Nor would I forget the thing she had become, but her cool hand wrapped around me before she impaled herself on my shaft.

Fuck.

I'd also not forgotten how good it felt inside of her, but my hands found Zacchaeus as she rolled her hips along my length.

It was an odd thing, to feel the resonance between us as Aurelia hit the height of ecstasy. Odder still to ride the waves of her euphoria to bring Zacchaeus to the edge over and over. Sometimes with my mouth, other times inside of me, and still others with my hand. Repeatedly bringing him right up to the brink before pausing, his deliciously urgent moans begging as I denied him the release he ached for.

Until, finally, I let him crash, his mouth between

Aurelia's legs as my hand gripped his twitching erection and my shaft pumped into him. He rode me through his ecstasy, until Aurelia and I came, nearly simultaneously. His heartbeat faded again as the music hit its bright chord and mellowed.

I placed Zacchaeus between myself and my former lover as the usual languor that follows suffused me. He had the audacity to giggle darkly at the arrangement as I threw an arm over my face.

"Good enough to fuck, but not good enough to sleep beside, eh?" He pressed a kiss to my jawline.

"She is no threat to me, but she is no love of mine."

"No love lost, my dear," she said. "But I'd be a fool to pass by an opportunity such as this."

I moved my arm and arched an eyebrow at her. "You think to make this a commonplace occurrence? Whatever happened to breaking me?"

"I have not taken you to my bed, dear Kristos. I have simply joined you in yours."

"Hmm." I put my arm back over my face.

"Besides," she purred, "this is much more fun."

There was a wet noise and she cried out again in pleasure. I moved my arm away again. Zacchaeus had his fingers between her legs, but watched me.

"Too much talking," he said with a roll of his shoulder.

I smiled and kissed him, our tongues dancing against each other as I reveled in the song dancing along my skin, until Aurelia exploded in ecstasy yet again.

This was a habit I was unsure I ever wanted to break.

TWENTY

ZACCHAEUS WAS NOT wrong when he said coteries were not peaceful. They were courts filled with intrigue, lies, and violence. Vampires do not readily trust one another and are unforgivingly ruthless. But with the werebear who had killed Longinus himself at his side, Zacchaeus' already considerable power and influence grew by leaps and bounds. His coterie and village became a new model for vampire life, though individual vampires had been keeping human sheep for centuries. Soon, vampires across the land had taken up the fashion of keeping entire villages of humans as communal livestock for their coterie.

It was strange to be a part of, strange to bear witness to, knowing that I was watching history unfold before me. But I could not help but wonder if perhaps the earthbound demons as a whole could be reasoned with and balanced alongside humanity much like a predator balances prey in an ecosystem.

Despite a multitude of opportunities over the course of nearly four hundred years, Aurelia had still not yet turned her first vampire. She took guidance from Zacchaeus, who wanted to carefully select the next member of the prestigious line of Firsts. But she was shrewd and powerful in her own right, though her temper was decidedly darker, her passions more flighty.

And the three of us had engaged in such wild adventures in the bedroom and beyond as to put the Kama Sutra to shame. To call the parties Zacchaeus held simple orgies was to downplay the sensuality and virility of those involved. Vampires have a strength and stamina that humans cannot hope to match, and I was even stronger still.

Certainly, in the centuries I had been among them, there had been werewolf incursions on Zacchaeus' coterie, but the wolves would never see the reason of what the vampires had created. They would not listen to the logic nor observe that the human livestock kept by the vampires were, in fact, healthier and longer-lived than their counterparts in other regions.

Finally, an ambitious young man from a moderately wealthy family fell into the coterie's lap. He was the third son, set to inherit virtually nothing when his parents passed. The thought of becoming nigh upon royalty if turned had him sleeping his way into Aurelia's bedroom, where she finally turned her first.

I could not watch her take his life, but she chuckled to herself as his body thumped to the ground. He hissed as he scrambled to his feet a moment later, clambering for the only creature in the room with a heartbeat. As I turned to defend myself from the threat, there was a sickening crack and Aurelia's limp body hit the floor. Zacchaeus held the new vampire by the throat, having apparently caught him before I had even turned, and I realized—with horror—that Zacchaeus had killed Aurelia. The new vampire struggled against Zacchaeus' firm grip.

The dark resonance between us trilled with a sort of charged excitement.

"NO!" I met his silver eyes. "Why would you do such a thing?!"

Zacchaeus held out a hand to me, restraining the struggling new vampire with the other. His voice was calm, patient. "Give me your arm, Kristos. Let this new one feed for a moment and all will be made clear."

I held his gaze. "You will explain first, Zacchaeus. She did not have to die."

"Of course she did." He tossed an errant curl from his forehead and reached for me again. "She would not be content with playing second fiddle to me forever. She was already growing too bold. Now, I won't have to watch for knives in my back," he tilted his head toward me. "Unless they come from you, of course. But you and I both know that will not happen. You're not built for it."

I did not move, nor take his hand. He tsked at me and bashed his elbow into the base of the new vampire's skull, sending him to the ground atop Aurelia's body.

"I guess I will simply have to bring him sustenance from the village," he said with a sigh and a shake of his head.

He looked back at me and closed the distance between us in a blink. The pad of his thumb traced across my cheek, erasing the trail a tear had carved there. "Do not cry for her, lover mine. She was always trying to break you. Now she will never have the chance."

He closed his mouth against mine, and I squeezed my eyes shut as the chord between us thrummed darkly. With a low growl, I pulled away from him, storming from the room.

The death of Aurelia was a revelation. With one sickeningly ruthless move, Zacchaeus had let his mask slip, undoing centuries of trust he had built with me. I had thought him different from the other earthbound demons. I had held him in higher regard, thinking his status as *consanguinea* had somehow insulated him from the dark machinations of turning vampire.

Zacchaeus had given me a place to belong and a purpose when mine had faltered. But I could not let stand the blatant evil I witnessed. A part of me still loved her, and that same part of me screamed for justice—or, at least, vengeance.

I ventured back to the church in the dead of winter, returning to the very grounds I had been excommunicated from. By some miracle, Brother Salathiel was still there, and he now led the wolves. I told him of Zacchaeus' manor, the coterie within, and the surrounding village of human livestock.

"I cannot give you proof of his demise," I told him. "But I can show you where his village lies and keep him in his manor until you arrive. His coterie is too large to take down on my own."

Salathiel nodded. "Leave now. I will send forces within a fortnight."

It was a coward's way out, but I knew I didn't possess the strength to do it myself. I made the two-week trek back to the village, and returned to the manor. In my cowardice, I avoided Zacchaeus as best I could, though I saw him here and there. I could not bear to speak to him, for fear I would tip him off to his imminent demise. To that end, I spent more time in the surrounding village than the manor itself, keeping company with the townsfolk in a half-hearted attempt to reconnect with a humanity I feared I had lost.

The church did not send the werewolves alone,

they sent what remained of the werebears too. The best the church knew, Zacchaeus was the oldest living vampire. They could not risk failure. They gathered outside the town at dawn and waited for the sun to rise. When it did, they barred all the doors and windows of the already shuttered manor before throwing torches atop the wooden roof.

The fire took hold immediately and spread quickly.

I never saw Zacchaeus leave.

In a flash of searing regret, I charged through a barred window on the first floor to try to save him. I realized too late I could never let Zacchaeus die. It was still as true as it had been the day he was turned outside the church gates. He had taken Aurelia from me, but she had long since stopped loving me.

He had not.

As I cast about from room to smoke-filled room, vampires reached for me, clawed at me to help them escape. But I wasn't here for them. I cursed myself. I had let my anger push me to finally take action on the order the church had given me centuries before, but my damned instinct to protect him hadn't kicked in until he was in mortal danger.

In my panic, I hadn't even noticed the music between us was distinctly silent. When I finally noticed its absence, I had reached his bedchamber. Our bedchamber. Or at least, what remained of it. The roof had collapsed, the boards of the floor above smoldering cinders where his bed should have been. I could smell nothing over the smoke, and even that was beginning to make me lightheaded.

I screamed my anguish at the hollow silence within me as I cast through what rooms still stood. I could not distinguish which ashen bodies were which among the destruction.

In resolute despair, I placed my back to a corner

on the bottom floor of the burning manor, sitting cross-legged on the flagstones, and let the smoke carry me to unconsciousness as tears of frustration, shame, and failure ran down my face.

TWENTY-ONE

MY HEART POUNDED. Zacchaeus had survived. He was alive. In a haze, I returned to my truck. I had to clear my head of him. Had to refocus. But he sparked an animalistic desire that would distract me until it was sated. And for the life of me, I couldn't even be angry about it. I grabbed my phone and searched for open bars. What I needed was only a couple more miles up the road. A short detour really. Surely the *purgatum* would be safe for a few more hours. I filled the truck's gas tank, started the engine, and drove.

A short while later, I stepped into the bar along the lonely stretch of highway. Heavy bass thumped in my chest as bodies writhed on the dance floor. Twinkle lights in repeated rainbows sparkled from the wooden rafters. They matched the flags nailed to the otherwise plain brick walls. I made my way across the floor to the bar, where I sat on the last empty stool.

I ordered a draft beer and took a slow sip of it as I turned to watch the writhing bodies on the dance floor. Most of the men here fell into one of two categories: big burly lumberjack types, or wiry lanky types. Either could have appealed to me, but I was looking for something much more specific. Something I was unlikely to find, really.

But I spotted something close. A lean man with bleached blond hair danced near the DJ. He had a bit of dark scruff on his face, but he was built of smooth muscle and danced as if it was all that brought joy to him in the world. He caught me watching him and I raised my beer at him. With a flirty smile, he made his way over to me.

He leaned close to my ear. "You look like the type to actually use those solid muscles of yours."

He smelled of tangy citrus. It wasn't exactly what I wanted, but I smiled at him anyway.

"I've been accused of knowing too well what to do with them," I replied in a dark growl, letting my nose brush his ear as I leaned close. "Buy you a drink?"

He pulled back with a radiant smile. "Maybe more than that." He ordered a mixed drink from the bartender before extending his hand to me. "I'm Paul."

I took his hand. "Kris."

He flashed his radiant smile at me again. "I hope you dance, Kris."

I downed the last of my beer as he grabbed his drink and let him pull me toward the dance floor. What passed for dancing these days was more grinding than anything, but I liked having his body pressed against mine as the bass thumped through the room, punctuated by tinny electronic sounds.

"I like your moves," he said thickly.

I let a little beast into my smile at the insinuation in his tone and the arousal threading through his scent.

"I think we should go somewhere a little more private, where you can show me how you really move." I punctuated the words with the press of my hips against his thigh.

He beamed at me. "I thought you'd never ask." He pressed his mouth to mine, tangling his fingers in my hair as I returned the kiss. The taste of the fruity mixed drink lingered on his tongue.

I reached down and brushed along his hips, moving my hand over to the hardening shaft in his pants. I gripped him through the fabric and pressed my body against him, reminding myself to be gentle, he was human. The corner of his mouth quirked up along with his eyebrow and he leaned into my hand, pressing the hardening shaft in his pants against my palm.

I pulled away from him. "You live close?"

He huffed out a laugh as we worked our way toward the door. "I *live* in Seattle. But I rented a cabin down the street."

"No strings." I smiled and brushed my lips against his again, feeling his smile against my mouth.

Out in the lot, he pulled me toward his silver SUV. I let him press my back to the vehicle as he kissed me again. I tried to let myself get lost in the taste of him, but I wanted more.

"I should follow you in my truck," I said against his mouth. "I have an early morning."

He batted dark lashes at me. "Hope that's not your way of ghosting me."

In a single move, I switched places with him, pressing him hard against the driver's side door of his SUV. It tore the wind from his lungs along with a truly delicious sound of pleasure and before he could suck in the next breath, I closed my mouth over his, pressing my thigh against the hardness in his pants.

His fingers closed into a tight grip of my shirt, and his startled noise turned to a groan of appreciation as I kissed him. He ground his hips against my thigh until I pulled away.

"Not ghosting," I told him. "I just don't want to leave until I absolutely have to."

"Mmmm." He licked his lips and looked me up and down. "Good."

"I'll follow you," I said, turning away and heading for my truck.

A little bit of highway, a handful of turns down half-paved roads, and a few minutes later, I pulled my truck alongside his SUV in front of a quaint little log cabin amidst the aspens and conifers of the forest.

"It's going to be a little chilly," he said as we approached the front door. "The owners asked me to turn off the heat every time I left. They don't wanna chance the heater starting a fire."

I nodded and pressed closer to him. "I can think of plenty of ways to keep warm in the meantime."

He closed his mouth against mine again, his tongue dancing with mine as he swung the door open and backed into the cabin.

We left a line of clothes from the front door to the bedroom, both of us eager to feel the other pressed against them. His skin was cool against my warmth, and though his tangy smell was all wrong and his movements lacked the grace I desired, he more than made up for it with his eagerness.

He slipped into me with the practiced ease of an experienced lover, and pumped against me until I gruffly pulled away from him, drawing a throaty whine from him. I laid down and lifted him onto my lap facing me, plunging into him and pumping against his ass as he rode me until his hot cum splattered onto my belly, drops of glistening white contrasting my tanned skin. It happened almost in slow motion, but then I pumped into him with nearly reckless abandon, my hand stroking his shaft hard again. I feared I nearly broke the boy, but he came again in my hand with a moan of ecstasy as I filled him with my own seed, a growl of appreciation rumbling from my chest.

"You *do* know all too well what to do with all those muscles," Paul said breathily, tracing a finger along my chest. "I'm glad I took the chance on you, Kris."

I laced my fingers behind my head. "Mmm. Me too." My eyelids drooped.

I blinked and Paul was asleep against my chest, his pale hair a mess. I glanced at the clock on the nightstand. It was a little past three in the morning. Dammit. The fatigue from the fight at the gas station had finally caught up to me. I had fallen asleep.

It was an imperfect scratch to the itch, but it certainly satisfied the urgency of it.

With a steady sigh, I peeled away from Paul and padded into the bathroom, where I relieved myself and drank some water from the sink. I quietly crept through the house, gathering both his and my clothes. When I got back to the bedroom, he was sitting up in bed.

"I thought you had left."

I smiled gently at him. "Not yet."

I started to pull on my shirt, but he rushed to stop me, his hand closing around my soft phallus.

"One more round?"

I was already hardening in his hand as he wrapped his mouth around the head of my cock.

Well, who was I to tell him no?

TWENTY-TWO

I left Paul dozing peacefully in his bed somewhere around four in the morning. Turns out his cabin was on the southeastern outskirts of Colorado Springs, just across I-25 from Fort Carson.

Zacchaeus was certainly too close to the *purgatum* for comfort, but I wasn't sure what to do about that yet. I drove into town, windows down so the cold breeze could clear my head and let me think.

But the sickening scent of vampire sent a thrill of anticipation down my spine. I drove more slowly, trying to pinpoint the scent.

There.

An alleyway with a covered entrance.

Red neon above the doorway read: The Chateau.

I pulled into a parking spot along the street as the desire for violence filled my veins. It was too late for there to be any casual club-goers left, and too early for the bleary-eyed bankers and office managers to be making their way through the streets. Anyone I ran into downtown at this time of morning was likely to be a vampire or sheep.

I remembered the *purgatum*'s voice on the phone. Her fear at what she was.

These earthbound demons were too close to her.

I took off my shirt and my boots, leaving them in the truck to stalk barefoot to the entrance of the club, the music still thumping out into the alleyway. I didn't care that it was November in Colorado. The chill in the air and the icy asphalt didn't faze me.

"Oh shit," the thick bouncer groaned. "Not again."

He reached for the cattle prod leaning against the doorframe, but I snapped his neck as his fingers gripped it.

There was a voice coming through the vampire's earpiece as he slumped to the ground. I smashed it along with his head with the heel of my foot, leaving a vaguely face-shaped pudding in cracked asphalt.

I picked up the cattle prod and took it with me as I kicked in the door. It'd come in handy if there were sheep who didn't want to leave.

The scents of sweat and alcohol, fog machine smoke and cigarettes assaulted my senses. But above it all was the sickening dead things scent of earth-bound demon.

A handful of humans writhed alongside a vampire on the dance floor. The sheep took no notice of the intrusion. The vampire rushed me.

I dropped the cattle prod, caught him around the neck, and suplexed him backwards into the ground, smashing his skull.

That apparently broke the spell for the sheep, who screamed and ran for the door.

Smart.

Five more bloodsuckers surrounded me as the dancers fled.

Dumb.

I dispatched them as easily as I had the vampires at the motel a few stops back, slamming their bodies into the support pillars for the upper balcony.

The bass of the music thumped in my chest as

their deaths sang a joyful chorus throughout my muscles. The upper balcony began a slow crumble to the dance floor, and I paused, inhaling deeply to pinpoint where to go next.

The back offices.

I eyed the cattle prod.

Fuck it.

I shifted to bear, the change taking me smoothly to four massive paws, and stalked toward the back office. There were two more vampires guarding the door beyond. Their skulls gave way beneath my paws with a wet crunch, and I threw my weight against the metal door. It warped and clanged open to hang uselessly from its hinges. Beyond that was a stairway down to a dark hallway with doors branching off at random intervals.

Down there, the scents of the club largely disappeared, leaving only the scents of death and decay.

Earthbound demons.

It made my mouth water with the desire to destroy this den.

One by one, I made my way through each and every door and hallway beneath the Chateau, killing any and every vampire I came across. By my count, there were thirty-seven of them, including the bouncer at the door and the six in the club. And all of the sheep I found were already dead. Ten dead humans, most of them women.

I crashed through every pillar and support pylon I found, intentionally crumbling the building. If the Chateau fell, the vampires would be forced to relocate. With any luck, they'd be smart enough to do it farther away from the *purgatum* than in the same fucking city.

At the end of the tunnel was a set of heavy metal doors, much like the ones that had led into these tunnels from the office. Outside air entered the mix of dead scents. I barreled through the doors to find one last vampire at the top of the stairs.

Thirty-eight.

The sheer terror filling his scent sang triumph throughout my body. His heart still beat from his last meal, its pace on par with a cornered rabbit.

"You may kill me," his panicked voice shook. "But you've never seen *anything* like Zacchaeus."

I suspect a smiling bear is terrifying, judging by the way the bloodsucker's fading heartbeat kicked into an even more frenzied tempo before I squelched his skull against the door frame.

Tossing his body aside, I shouldered through that door and into a storage room. Another set of metal double doors was set into the far wall, and there were tinted windows high in the surrounding walls, cracked open to let in the brisk morning air. I pushed open the far doors and out onto the concrete stage of a small amphitheater on the edge of a city park.

As I scented my way back toward the Chateau and my truck, cement dust filled the air along with the tang of short-circuiting electricity.

I swear it was like a fucking choir of angels coursing through me.

I had succeeded. The Chateau was reduced to rubble.

Only now there were military vehicles surrounding the area, blocking my truck into the space I'd pulled into.

Fuck.

There was no point trying to be stealthy. Bears are big, and I was bigger still.

That didn't stop the pasty blond guy with wire rimmed glasses from shooting me with... a tranq gun? This dumbass really thought I was an *actual* bear?

I huffed out a growl and swatted the neon green

fluff of the needle from my fur. I charged the idiot, whose back was to my truck, eyeing the area as I did.

No one else around. Good.

His eyes widened behind his glasses as I shifted smoothly back to two legs just steps from him and continued to charge him, grabbing him by his collar and lifting him from the ground as I got in his face. I didn't give a shit that the asshole was taller than me.

Except he was a werewolf. What the fuck did he even wear the glasses for?

Heavy footsteps picked their way around the rubble at the edges of the fallen club.

"Put him down, pup, we're on the same side." The gruff voice behind me had the same tone as the police officer in Texas. Another one accustomed to his authority being recognized as law.

I shook my head as I turned around, lazily tossing the lean werewolf at the feet of a stocky man past his prime. They wore matching army fatigues.

A commanding officer then. The tag on his right breast read Buckheim.

"Bear," the pale one said by way of correction as he stood and readjusted his glasses. His nametag read Langley.

Buckheim harrumphed noncommittally.

I studied the stocky commander. He was just as much werewolf as Langley was. And he was old. Probably one of the oldest werewolves still kicking, judging by the grey in his hair and the wrinkles on his face. Since when did the American military have fucking werewolves?

"Same side of a good fight?" I jerked my head toward the rubble of the Chateau. "Then I'm sure you understand why that needed to fall."

Buckheim crossed his arms. "You expect me to believe that was all you?"

Well, this wasn't a conversation I was interested in having while naked. Or at all, really.

I turned and opened the door to my truck. "You can believe it or not. Makes no difference to me." I pulled a pair of sweatpants from my bag and sat on the seat to pull them on. The fatigue from the fight started to weigh on me.

"One wolf isn't capable of that kind of destruction," he said.

I blew out a breath. "That's rich. Give a wolf enough time to plan and a strategic supply of demolitions and he could make it happen."

"He's not a wolf," Langley insisted.

Buckheim arched an eyebrow at him and looked back at me.

I crossed my arms and jerked a chin at him. "U.S. Army, huh? Who calls the shots for your pack?"

"You don't have the clearance," Langley spat.

Buckheim shot him a look and replied, "I do."

He wasn't lying.

"Good," I nodded. "Then your report should read something like 'particularly motivated werewolf takes down vampire den in downtown Colorado Springs.'"

Buckheim steeled his expression. "Should it now?"

There was power rising to meet his frustration.

I blinked at him. He was the alpha of whatever counted for a pack in the military. Shouldn't have been surprising, all told.

"Demolitions weren't used here." Buckheim's gruff voice was cool and matter-of-fact.

"Nope."

"When did bears become part of the equation?"

I arched an eyebrow at him before meeting Langley's steely eyes. "You don't have the clearance." I hooked a thumb toward my tailgate. "Move the Jeep."

"Or what?" Langley held my gaze. Ballsy pup.

I sighed and paced over to the front of the flat beige military vehicle. Lifting the front bumper of the Jeep until the wheels came off the road, I moved it out of the way, setting it down gently when it was clear. I padded back to the driver's side of my truck, climbed in, and shut the door.

"Keep fighting the good fight, pups." I waved a hand out the window as the engine rumbled to life.

Miraculously, they didn't try to stop me a second time as I pulled away from the destroyed nightclub.

TWENTY-THREE

COLORADO SPRINGS, NOVEMBER 2019

NEARLY TWENTY MINUTES LATER, I arrived at the ruins of the last address I'd had for Sheppard. I pressed my lips into a line. The house here had burnt down and was surrounded by caution tape. A backhoe sat in the yard, a silent sentinel waiting to clear the land.

I pulled my phone from my pocket and thumbed through the contacts until I got to Sheppard.

"Took you long enough, Pack-killer," he said, his voice groggy with sleep.

I couldn't help but smile at the friendly use of the nickname I had rightfully earned so long ago. "Yeah, yeah, Alpha. Just give me the address I'm actually supposed to be at instead of this burnt-out husk of your old place."

He yawned. "I'll text it to you. See you soon."

The line went dead, but my phone buzzed a moment later with the new address. I saved it before pulling up the map on my phone. Same neighborhood, a couple of streets over.

A few minutes later, I pulled along the street across from a modern, boxy home big enough to house a pack twice the size I'd last seen Sheppard running with. There were tall bushes planted around the property line to lend a semblance of privacy that the house's otherwise enormous windows wouldn't. The scents of the pack drifted on the breeze as I noted the vehicles in the driveway—a couple of cars, one white and one blue, parked bumper to bumper next to a black Dodge Ram. The truck had easy entrance and egress from the driveway.

Must be Sheppard's.

Though sunrise was still easily an hour and a half away, the scents of the night were already beginning to give way to the dawn. I pulled a shirt from my bag along with a pair of socks and pulled them on. My boots followed, though I didn't bother to tie them—I simply tucked my laces in.

The door to the mostly glass house swung open as I shut my truck door. Sheppard's muscular build filled the doorway, his sandy blond hair still disheveled from sleep.

He extended a hand with a smile as I approached. "Been a while, Pack-killer."

I returned the smile and pulled him into a hug, slapping his shoulder. "Plenty long enough, Alpha."

Over his shoulder, I spotted the milky and brown eyes set into an all-too-familiar face.

"Holy hell, the hot-head's still alive!" I extended a hand to Matt, whose blond hair was shorter and less shaggy than he'd kept it before.

Matt rolled his eyes at me and took my hand, shaking it once before releasing it. "At least some of us get better with age."

I snorted at him as Sheppard stepped back from the door, inviting me in with a gesture. Three other werewolves sat on couches in the living room—two females and a male. One of the ladies—the freckled one with the curly red-brown hair—smelled like Matt. The other smelled like the male sitting next to her, and vice versa. She had long blonde hair and crystal-blue eyes, while her mate had dark brown hair with dark eyes to match. They all watched me with skeptical expressions.

"I don't think you know any of the rest of my pack these days," Sheppard said.

"It's only been a hundred years or so," I replied. "Your whole pack turn over in that time?"

Sheppard shook his head and sighed, but Matt's musky scent spiked.

"You saw him after that bullshit with the church packs during the revolution?"

Sheppard eyed the scarred wolf. "You think I pulled the information out of thin air about those vamps in New York a century back? Sit down. This is why I didn't tell you."

Power washed through the room, stronger than I'd felt from him in the past. He had a strong pack these days. Good.

Matt closed his mouth with a scowl, crossed his arms, and sat on the arm of the couch next to the curly haired wolf. She watched me with shrewdly calculating hazel eyes as she laid a hand on Matt's thigh. His scent lost its edge as he let out a sigh.

Sheppard gestured to the curly haired lady. "That's Chastity, Matt's mate."

She held my gaze and nodded a greeting.

"And on the other couch," he continued, "is Daniel and his mate, Kaylah."

Daniel smiled as he stood and extended a hand to me. I shook it firmly before taking Kaylah's offered hand and touching it gently.

A door opened in the downstairs hallway and a lanky beanpole of a wolf with short brown hair sticking up in all directions padded over to Kaylah and Daniel's couch, slumping into the corner cushion and leaning sleepily against Kaylah's shoulder. He wore only a pair of black sweatpants, and scars ripped across his right shoulder down to his stomach.

Sheppard smiled as Kaylah ruffled the wolf's hair. "That's Jamie."

Jamie squinted pale green eyes at me. "Hey, man."

He looked as tired as I felt.

"He's the younger brother of one of my other wolves," Sheppard said. "His brother's name is Jonathan. He and Lynn should be on their way here, along with Ian."

Kaylah kissed Daniel's temple and stood. "I'll go'n git th' coffee on."

"Good call," Daniel said as she stepped into the kitchen.

Sheppard arched a wry eyebrow at me. "I had to ask that cop who called what the hell he meant by 'Sweetwater PD.' I thought it was some kind of wrong number situation, until he mentioned he had a 'Chris' there who'd brought up my name in con-nection with a blue Ford F-150."

I smiled at him. "It was better than trying to ex-plain to him I couldn't get a driver's license and thus couldn't register a car."

"You know, we can get a modern identity up and running for you so you don't have to deal with that mess." Daniel offered, throwing his arm over the back of the couch. He crossed his right leg over his left, a movement that was comically out of place in his sweatpants.

A modern identity? That'd only make it that much easier for the church to realize I hadn't died when they razed Zacchaeus' manor.

No, thank you.

"Speaking of cops," I said to Sheppard. "What do you know of some long-in-the-tooth army alpha named Buckheim? Hangs with a pasty blond named Langley?"

"Buckheim's an ally," Sheppard replied, though there was something unsaid there. "The other's one of his lackeys. Why?"

"I had a run in with the two of them when he was investigating the collapse of the vampire den downtown."

Sheppard jerked his chin at me. "That where you got those scratches?"

I touched my cheek. I had forgotten they were there. Forgotten I don't heal wounds from Zacchaeus in my usual blink.

"Wait," Chastity said as the scent of coffee filled the air. "The vampire den downtown? The Chateau? It collapsed?"

"Too many vampires too close to your *consanguinea*," I said. "Can't have that."

"I would have paid cold hard cash to see that asshole's face," Chastity said.

Sheppard crossed his arms and power washed through the air. The wolves on the couches sat up straighter, eyeing me, some more blearily than others. Even Kaylah moved to where she could see me from the kitchen.

I pressed my lips into a line. I was way the fuck too tired to fight a whole wolf pack that jumped to conclusions.

"You're here for Lynn, aren't you?" Sheppard crossed his arms over his chest. "I thought you were separated from the church."

I blew out a breath. "I am. I'm only here to keep her safe."

Matt stood and shook a finger at me. "Oh no, asshole. That's *not* number three. She is plenty safe without you!"

"Matthew!" The tone of Sheppard's voice held a warning.

I tried not to let my smile taunt the hot-head too much, but riling him was all too easy.

"I could no sooner ignore her presence than I could take my own life." I looked at Sheppard. "I have not forgotten that your pack is owed one more favor. I suspect it should be much easier to reach me should you have need in the coming years."

TWENTY-FOUR

OUTSIDE, the rumble of an engine drew close and then shut off. Sheppard looked to the front door as a familiar warmth filled my veins. I held my breath as the brightness of it flowed into me.

And then the door opened and the chord sang through me, brighter than I remembered it from before. Once more, it was like the holy light of heaven itself poured directly into my bloodstream.

Two more wolves stepped into the house. A male and a female.

The male had shoulder-length dark hair and wore a black hooded jacket over a t-shirt and loose jeans.

The other wolf was the *purgatum*.

She had wavy brown hair to her mid-back and large, stormy grey eyes. She wore a long white t-shirt under her brown leather jacket, and had on grey leggings that tucked into her fuzzy boots. She met my gaze and immediately glanced away, almost like she'd hoped I hadn't been watching her come in.

The sight of her sucker-punched me in the gut. The same instinct that had caused me to drive across the entire damn country to get to her screamed at me to take her far from this place—far from Zacchaeus, far from the reach of any military organizations that would want to use her, far from the Catholic church.

And yet, I could do none of those things without having to fight the whole pack to make it happen. And she'd probably hate me for it.

Unless... I could convince them to leave too. They didn't need to stay anyway, not now that the Chateau had fallen.

"Kristos," Sheppard said, breaking my train of thought. "This is Jonathan, Jamie's brother."

Jonathan shook my hand with mischief in his lopsided smile.

"And, as I'm sure you've guessed, that's Lynn, our *consanguinea*."

She tilted her head quizzically to the side as she looked at me without meeting my gaze.

Being in her presence was like a tuning fork had been struck and laid against my skin, a not entirely unpleasant sensation. It was as if I had been walking through life off-key, as if I were a note falling flat. This close to her, the world became more clear, more vibrant. Everything sharpened, and my purpose flowed through me like a whisper of silk.

I was created to protect her.

"The *purgatum*," I breathed.

I reached a hand to greet her, but stopped myself, remembering what a *purgatum* is capable of. Could she turn even one such as I human again? Would I turn to dust instead, like an earthbound demon might?

The corner of her mouth quirked and she extended her hand to meet mine. "It's fine, Kristos. I think you hit the nail on the head when you said I had to want it."

Her warm hand settled against my palm.

"I am deeply humbled and honored to make your acquaintance, my dear." I covered her hand with my own in reverence. Her pulse pounded, sending a bright chord thrumming through my muscles like a Tibetan prayer bowl.

"It's good to have a face to match the voice on the phone." She smiled gently but tried not to meet my eyes.

I cocked my head to the side and watched her. There was no fear in her heady wildflower scent, and no lie to her words. Still I could not shake that she was decidedly nervous of me.

This resonance with her was unlike anything I had felt with Zacchaeus. It was bright and full and strong and nearly burned in my veins in a way that was not at all unpleasant.

The electric scent that had joined that of the pack sharpened as I held her hand and I glanced at Jonathan. Her sweet scent clung to him.

Oh I see.

She is spoken for.

I patted the back of her hand once and released it with a gentle smile of my own.

"Coffee's ready," Kaylah called from the kitchen, breaking the spell.

I blinked as Lynn hooked an arm in Jonathan's and they stepped into the kitchen. The pack didn't say anything as they all filled their mugs with varying levels of coffee, honey, and milk. I smiled as Lynn skipped the milk altogether and poured a truly unholy amount of honey into her coffee.

The pack settled around the black granite slab of a dining table with their mugs of coffee, and I joined them with my own mug. It would keep the press of the fatigue at bay a little while longer. Though a nap was becoming inevitable.

The *purgatum*'s eyes were trained on my chest, her expression thoughtful. "Why does the world feel safer now that you're here?"

Finally, she met and held my gaze.

The electric scent in the air sharpened.

Jonathan set his jaw at the edges of my vision.

"Well, Peter always said we were to be the biggest brothers *consanguinea* ever had," I said.

She arched an eyebrow at me. "Peter? Peter who?"

"*The* Peter," I replied as I took a slow first sip of my coffee. "Jesus' apostle. The one who created the werebears."

Sheppard leaned an elbow on the table. "Now that's a story I hadn't heard."

"Of course not," I said. "You wolves were created over three hundred years later." When they excommunicated me for not killing my charge-turned-vampire. The music in my veins darkened for a heartbeat, almost reaching the minor chord that matched my recollection of Zacchaeus.

"Tell us about it?" Lynn asked.

I tapped my fingers against my mug, considering her suggestion, and looked at her. She nodded once, slowly.

She was distracting me.

She felt the melody between us just as Zacchaeus had.

I tilted my mug toward her in thanks and took another long sip of my coffee.

"There's not a lot to tell," I said finally. "About twenty-five or thirty years after Jesus was crucified, Peter created the werebears from the holy relics of the crucifixion."

"I heard it was werewolves," Sheppard said.

"Of course you did." I shook my head. "But your kind doesn't date back that far. Peter started with us bears, and we weren't nearly as numerous."

"Hmm." Chastity held her mug in both hands, her elbows on the table. She looked over Sheppard's face and hands once and then rested her hazel eyes on me.

I pressed my lips into a line as she watched me as a scientist might examine a new species from afar, clearly comparing me to her alpha.

I furrowed my brow at her and turned to Sheppard. "Might I make use of your shower?"

Sheppard smiled as he stood. "Sure. You look like you could use a nap too."

I nodded. "I'm built to berserk and rest."

"I'd say y'earnt it," Kaylah said, smiling at me over the rim of her coffee mug.

Sheppard showed me where the shower was upstairs. After a quick rinse, I threw my sweatpants and shirt back on. The fatigue suffused my limbs after the warmth of the shower, and I laid on the couch in the upstairs den, ignoring the chatter of the wolves downstairs. The light of dawn began to stream through the window. As I drifted off to sleep, I marveled at the strength and power of the resonance between Lynn and myself.

TWENTY-FIVE

ATHENS, WINTER 60

I WAS BORN the day Jesus was crucified. I grew up in Athens, a city history refuses to forget, for better or for worse. My father was a jeweler, and he taught me to take up the profession as I grew into adulthood. I was a young man of sixteen when the apostle Paul came to Athens, proselytizing the teachings of Jesus. I was as moved by his words as my father was, and our house began to follow the Christian God, ceasing our previous tributes to the Greek gods. The next summer, I married the woman I had spent all my days pining for since my fourteenth year. My wife, Myrrhine, blessed me with three beautiful children—my thoughtful and kind son, Anatolius, and my mischievous twin daughters, Caelina and Marcellina.

And in the dead of winter of my twenty-seventh year, the earthbound demons took them all from me.

Three of them burst into our house late at night, hissing at the crosses we had taken to keeping in the windows and on the door. It was a custom most of us had by that time, as we learned that crosses were one of very few things that could hurt them. The larger of the three grabbed and held me while the other two destroyed my family. They tore my children limb from limb in front of me, laughing at their screams as they lapped and slurped at their blood. They raped my wife, holding her down with fingers that scraped gashes along her arms and legs before bleeding her dry. I screamed and shouted my anger and anguish as I lunged at them, trying to tear myself from the iron grip of the one who held me. But he simply laughed as he raked his nails along my sides and back, dropping me as the loss of blood made me weak. I fell into unconsciousness as I lay face to face with my wife's unblinking eyes, my body curled around the mangled heap that had been my son.

I woke screaming days later in a church common room, surrounded by others with ailments and injuries of varying severity. Nuns nursed me back to health, and gave me milk of the poppy when the nightmarish visions of that night returned to me. They sent priests to pray with me when I was awake and to pray for my soul while I slept. I woke for the dawn, shed tears for the sunset, slept in the starlight, and prayed the nightmares would take me from this world. I did not dare try to take my own life, for fear I would never be able to reunite with my once-beautiful family in heaven.

My prayers went unheard.

I had failed my family. I had no one to carry on my legacy.

So when word reached me that Peter was looking for strong Christian men who would fight against the foul creatures, I could do aught but seize the opportunity. I had nothing to lose.

As it turned out, none who made it through the ritual did. Barely a handful of the volunteers even survived.

Peter had asked us to dedicate our lives to protecting the children of Mary, the bloodline of the brothers and sisters of Jesus, the *consanguinea*. We swore to sacrifice our safety, our bodies, and our very lives to keep the children of the blood safe from the earthbound demons.

In return, we became stronger, faster, more attuned to the world around us. The ritual Peter had found tapped into a divinity that has only been seen once since, when the werewolves were created. But even they were lesser copies of us. Our very souls had been connected to the bears sacrificed with honor to the cause.

It broke each of us, tore us from the humanity we had once known and then returned us to it anew. We did not know then that part of the cost had been a portion of our free will. I, for one, did not care, and I suspect the others were equally unconcerned. I finally had the power to make the vampires pay for killing my children, for defiling my wife, for destroying aught I held dear.

As we woke from the slumber of recovery, Peter presented each of us with a small wooden cross hung on a leather cord. Each one had been carved from the wood of the very cross Jesus had been crucified with. Each hummed faintly with the presence of the divine within them. He named us brothers then, and the church became our home.

Had I ever questioned our family's choice to convert years before, the very real power I held within me would have banished all doubt.

TWENTY-SIX

When I woke, the sunlight was streaming in through my window, bright and glaring. And with it, the melody of the *purgatum* breathed through me like a whisper. She was still at the house then. The smell of roasted meat and potatoes with rosemary and garlic made my mouth water. I looked at my phone. It was half past four in the afternoon. I wiped sleep from my eyes, savoring the scent of the cooking meal, and just listened to the vibrant chord quietly flowing throughout my body.

There were voices outside, behind the house. Shouts and laughter.

After a moment, I stood to look out the window. Sheppard's pack darted around in his backyard, tumbling over each other like puppies while a football got passed around. It made me smile. The warmth of Sheppard's pack was infectious.

I grabbed my boots and headed downstairs, the music within me deepening as the world sharpened around me like a set of binoculars coming into focus. But instead of putting my boots on, I stepped out to throw them and socks into my truck, the chords dulling again as I moved farther away from the backyard. Since I hadn't had any sort of plan when coming here, it hadn't occurred to me to check for nearby lodging.

I looked back at the house.

I wasn't sure distance between us was a good idea anyway with a First like Zacchaeus so close.

Why hadn't he made a move yet?

He had to know she was here and what she was capable of. The vamps she dusted less than a week ago were almost certainly from his coterie.

Then again, Zacchaeus had a patience that rivaled my own. He wouldn't make a move until he was certain he could manufacture exactly the outcome he wanted.

Which was bad news for Sheppard and his pack.

Fuck.

I sighed and paced barefoot around to the backyard, heedless of the November chill.

As I got closer to the pack, closer to Lynn, the world sharpened like clearing a drunken stupor and the chord singing in my veins became an unignorable elation.

And on its heels? The warm peace of Sheppard's pack, a sharp contrast to the relatively unstable packs I'd seen him try to hold together in the past. Sampson had been a stabilizing force for the pack a few centuries ago, but he had been one wolf in a small pack. These days, Sheppard clearly had more than that.

"I had forgotten you sleep like the dead," Sheppard said, noticing my arrival. "I sent Kaylah to wake you for lunch, but you wouldn't budge."

I shrugged. "Comes with the territory."

"Some protector," Matt snapped.

"I'd have known if Lynn was in danger."

From across the yard, her attention snapped to me.

"Oh?" Sheppard tossed the football to Matt.

I nodded once as she approached and looked back at the alpha. "She and I are connected. If she were in trouble, that connection would wake me."

"Connected?" Jonathan's gold-flecked green eyes narrowed at me as he crossed his arms. He took a step in her direction, nearly placing himself between her and me.

He might as well have shouted 'back off asshole, she's mine' at me.

I sighed. "I was built to protect *consanguinea*. So, I always seem to know when I'm close to one. I can feel it. And if they're in trouble, I feel that too. Like an alarm."

I hadn't ever tried to explain the resonance to anyone. At least, no one that I didn't already share it with. It was hard to put into words.

"Hmm," Sheppard mused. "Well, Ian got here while you were asleep." He gestured to a skinny young wolf with short brown hair and sapphire eyes.

"Nice to meet ya." Ian smiled and extended his hand.

I shook it, nodding once in greeting.

The football slammed into my chest, and I grabbed it as it bounced off.

"Join in, Pack-killer," Matt said. "Let's see what you got."

The nickname held considerably more vitriol coming from his mouth. Sheppard used the name with wry amusement; Matt used it with long-simmering anger.

I shook my head and tossed the ball back to Matt. He snatched it from the air one-handed.

"I don't play," I told him.

Sheppard raised an eyebrow.

"C'mon man," Jonathan said, throwing his head back in exasperation. "You've been dead to the world for hours!"

I peered at him, but his face was full of mirth.

Matt shrugged and tossed the football to Lynn, who eyed me and thumped the football against my chest. Her heart pounded, adding a nervous cadence to the light thrumming through my muscles.

"Gotta let loose sometime," she said.

I pressed my lips into a line and tossed the ball to Sheppard before turning back to her.

"I'm not a wolf," I said. "I don't play by pack rules."

She held my gaze, the challenge dancing with cautious mirth on her face. "Show me."

There was no missing Sheppard's smile at the edge of my vision. A playful tension wound through the pack.

I sighed. Now was not the time to try to talk to them about Zacchaeus.

Fuck.

"Fine." I surveyed the wolves. Nine in total. Couple of lanky beanpole types, a handful of ladies, and a couple of bigger wolves. Then there was Jonathan and Daniel, whose average build likely belied the strength of their wolf.

Sheppard tossed the ball to Jonathan, who passed it to Kaylah before the pack could get to him.

"Two simple rules," Sheppard said as Kaylah dodged around Matt and Ian before passing the ball to Lynn. "Don't let the ball hit the ground." Lynn passed the ball to Sheppard, who held it firm until the pack piled on him.

Jonathan smiled as he offered a hand to his alpha. "And get rid of the ball before you're dogpiled."

A corner of my mouth quirked up.

Lynn kissed his cheek with a laugh. "Nice. *Dog*piled."

He chuckled, the sound rumbling in his chest as he turned and gave her a deeper kiss. She melted into it, the harmony between us singing her joy, and placed her hand against his chest. She cut off the kiss with a sly grin, snatched the ball from his hand, and threw it to Jamie.

The game resumed.

Jamie threw the ball across the yard to Daniel, who dodged Chastity and Sheppard before tossing it to Matt. Matt threw it at me, and I caught it, mirroring Sheppard's tactic of holding it firm as the pack's weight slammed into me from all sides.

Only they couldn't take me to the ground.

At least, not immediately. But then one of them wrapped around my left leg while another crouched against the back of my right. A couple more helped pull my left leg out from under me as Matt shouldered my chest, sending me to the ground over the back of the wolves behind my right leg.

I guffawed out a laugh as I hit the ground. I had never played any game with wolves. I had sparred with them in the past, sure, but never more than three at a time. This was an entirely novel experience.

Didn't mean I was ready to let them have their ball back.

I'm not pack, after all.

I curled around my grip on the ball and let the pack scrabble at me. After a moment of struggle, power washed through the air and the wolves peeled themselves from the pile.

"Alright old bear," Sheppard said, arms crossed. "Don't ignore the rules just because you can." There was a smile playing at his mouth.

I raised an eyebrow and grinned as I tossed him the ball. "I said I wasn't wolf."

Sheppard tossed the ball to Lynn, who caught it and smiled at me. She lobbed it over my head to Matt.

"New rule," Matt said. "Don't let the bear have the ball." He passed it to Chastity, his mate.

Her face lit with joy as she took a few steps back to analyze the pack and me. "Now we have a game." She tossed the ball across the yard to Ian.

Indeed we did.

The other rules clearly still applied, as the pack stalked toward Ian. He grinned as he searched the tail end of the pack. The ball sailed over their heads toward Jamie, who quickly passed it to Sheppard again.

This time, I joined the pack in stalking the alpha, but he ran toward us all, throwing the ball straight up into the air as he did.

Rule one: don't let the ball hit the ground.

Jamie was a couple of inches taller than the rest of the pack, so he grabbed it out of the air and ran to clear himself before lobbing it back toward Lynn.

She caught it, but was standing right next to Jonathan, who took out her legs and landed on top of her, the two of them giggling as he reached out and pulled Kaylah into the pile for no discernable reason. But she laughed along with them anyway as she went down.

Rule two: get rid of the ball before you're dogpiled.

The ball popped up into the air again, and as I reached for it, Matt smacked it away and Daniel got a grip on it before it hit the ground, crouching low and then recovering once he had it. His body was turned toward Lynn, who had cleared herself from Jonathan's tackle and was watching him with Jamie and Kaylah nearby, and prepped to throw the ball to one of them.

But his eyes watched Ian on the far side of the yard. So, when the ball sailed that direction, I plucked it out of the air and held it firm as the pack piled into me again.

Rule three: don't let the bear get the ball.

The joy singing through the resonance filled my heart and matched the energy flowing through the pack as Lynn's laughter rang out again. She and Kaylah pushed me over Jonathan, who had crouched low behind my left leg, as Matt yanked my right leg out from under me. I lost my grip on the football as I went down again.

When I looked up, Sheppard had the ball. He smiled at me. "Looks like bears play just fine."

Jonathan laughed as he pulled himself out from under me. "Now *that's* woofball!"

I furrowed my brow at him as Lynn's laughter deepened to a full belly laugh.

Woofball.

Woof.

Like the sound dogs make.

That's fucking hilarious.

"I'm still not calling it that," Matt said as Sheppard tossed him the ball.

"You should, hot-head," I said as laughter took me. "It's an apt name!"

Jonathan clapped me on the shoulder, laughing with me as he gripped my forearm. I didn't need his help getting up, but the camaraderie was a nice touch.

"Some old farts are just set in their ways," he said.

TWENTY-SEVEN

I PLAYED with the pack for a while longer before the incessant whine of a timer rang out from the kitchen of the glass house.

"Welp," Kaylah drawled. "Dinner time, y'all!"

A short while later, after handwashing and the retrieval of an extra chair for me from the basement, the pack was seated around the black granite slab of a dining room table, adding slices of roasted meat and spoonfuls of cut potatoes to their plates. Some slathered butter onto rolls before digging in.

I waited for the pack to get their portions before getting my own. I was the guest in a wolf pack's home, after all. Still, my diet was not as meat-heavy as theirs. As such, my plate held more potatoes than meat, along with a couple of rolls.

Kaylah eyed my dinner. "Ain'tcha like th' roast?"

"On the contrary." I smiled at her as I took a bite. "It's delicious. I just eat less meat than you wolves do."

"Well whaddya eat 'nstead?"

I rolled a shoulder. "Usually fruit more than meat, sometimes eggs or beans instead. Whatever's easy."

"Mmm," she mused. "Well'n I'll go'n git ya sum n'uh mornin'. We're low on honey anyhow."

I shook my head as I swallowed the bite of potato I'd taken. "Not necessary. I'll take care of myself."

Sheppard took another bite of his roast. "You're staying here while you're in town, aren't you?"

"I hadn't gotten that far yet," I admitted. "Coming here wasn't exactly in the plan."

"So you aren't with the church then?" Lynn poked at the food on her plate as the chord between us darkened. "You're not here to try to cart me off to the Vatican?"

A perfectly justified fear, really. The darkness in the music between us made my heart ache.

Damn this purpose of mine.

I gave her a wry laugh. "Not unless you wanna rub in their face how they shouldn't have any say in what your future holds."

Sheppard put a hand atop hers. "I told you it was unlikely he'd go back to the church. That's why I called him."

I snorted. "Those fuckers excommunicated me ages ago. They've clearly lost all record of my existence by now." Or at least, I hoped they had. The church had certainly been gone from my life long enough to suggest so.

Sheppard eyed me. "So you're really here to be a bodyguard for a *consanguinea* who already has a pack that will protect her without question?"

I took a sip of my water. "She's more than even your everyday *consanguinea*, and you know it as well as the rest of your pack does. Like I said on the phone, the church killed the last *purgatum*—the only one I'd ever known of before her. I may not have planned to come here, but I'm damn glad I did. You pups are in deeper shit than you know."

"We're not afraid of the church," Matt snapped.

"Or the military," Sheppard added.

I put my fork down. "That's great, but you *should* be scared of the First hiding out in your territory. He's almost assuredly caught wind of her."

A trill went through the melody in my veins, something cold singing into the notes.

"First?" Lynn's voice was quiet.

"Vampire royalty," I explained. "The first vampire turned of the first turned all the way back to Longinus himself."

"Like *consanguinea*," Sheppard said.

I nodded. "Only vampires. Powerful fucks who throw their weight around like a vamp ten times their age. And you have one right in your backyard."

They quieted, taking that in for a moment. Nine wolf hearts beat a syncopated rhythm around the table. Two of them beat in time to the thrumming of the resonance—the *purgatum*, of course, and her lover.

"So what do we do?" Jamie asked, breaking the silence.

"Normally, you'd want to band together and hit the fucker as hard as you could. Nuke it from orbit, if you had the ordinance."

Chastity leveled her shrewd gaze at me. "But…?"

"But you don't stand a chance against this one. He's probably one of the oldest vampires still walking the Earth."

She leaned her elbows on the table. "How old does that make him, exactly?"

"About seventeen hundred years old, give or take a couple years."

Chastity sat back as Matt whistled.

"How do you know that?" Lynn asked. The music between us turned icy, running cold fingers down my spine.

"Because I was there when he was turned."

Matt's palms hit the table. "And you didn't stop it?" His tone was incredulous.

I balled a fist and met his eyes. Eye. Though the milky one threatened to stare right through me as well. I gritted my teeth and forced my voice to stay even and controlled as the guilt roiled through me and tried to make me roar. "It was an ambush. They got to him before I could stop them."

Sheppard stood, and I felt the power rush through the pack. The melody sharpened and warmed as the wolves relaxed back in their chairs.

"Just how old does that make you, Kristos?" Sheppard's voice was nearly a whisper.

I couldn't help the rueful smile that spread across my face. So I looked away, watching the clouds pick up the colors of the sunset sky through the window. "I was born the day Jesus was crucified. Humanity has changed calendars enough that I'm not sure anymore exactly how many years ago that is."

Lynn gasped, and I glanced her way. She stared at me, her eyes wide. Next to her, Jonathan's eyes were just as wide. As were Jamie's next to him. As were all of the wolves as I looked at each in turn. Chastity's hand was over her mouth, which was agape with awe.

Well, shit. None of them had ever met anything so old.

Fuck me.

Lynn broke the silence, her eyebrow raised at her alpha. "But Sheppard, you said the oldest werewolf you knew was around eight hundred years old."

"I did." Sheppard nodded. "And it's still true. I never knew how old Kristos was, and—even if I had known—he's not a werewolf."

"Well'n it's no wonder y'hand'd Buckheim his ass." Kaylah took another bite of her roast, seemingly determined to go back to business as usual.

"We always were stronger than the werewolves."

Jonathan poked at his potatoes. "We?"

"You don't really think I'm the only werebear Peter made, do you?"

"I think you're the only one left." Sheppard tore off a piece of his roll and popped it into his mouth.

My face went slack. I hadn't seen any werebears in… a very long time. And last I heard, the church had been choosing recklessness with what was left of my brethren.

"That part is probably true, old friend. It has been centuries since I last saw another of my kind." I moved the bits of potato and roast on my plate around with my fork.

The silence stretched as the pack resumed their meal, forks scraping against plates. I tried to do the same, but the reminder of the guilt surrounding Zacchaeus and the sad thought that I was very likely the last of my brethren stole my appetite.

The chord rang darkly against my skin. I glanced at Lynn again. Sadness touched her expression. Beside her, Jonathan held her hand but watched me as his electric scent grew sharper.

I sighed and pressed my lips into a line as I looked away. He was so damn smitten with her, and she with him, they might as well be mates already. Lord knows they were headed that way.

"Nearly two thousand years old and still fit as a fiddle," Chastity said, drawing my attention.

I nodded, sitting back in my chair and crossing my arms as she watched me. Once again, I felt like a specimen being analyzed.

"You've watched empires rise and fall, seen all of the world's major wars, and watched plague after plague decimate the world's population."

"The vampires were behind most of those," I said. "They hoped if there were less people, it'd be easier to control them. And they hoped the wolves were susceptible as well. Thank God they were wrong."

"Why'd they switch from bears to wolves anyway?" Chastity sounded like a fascinated historian.

She did have a veritable living piece of history right in front of her, after all.

I sighed and counted the points on my fingers. "You're better at taking orders. You pack-bond. You work together." I put my hand down. "And your co-operation is an instinctively-coordinated harmony that is decidedly more artful than the brute force of my brethren. But it was mostly because you're better at taking orders." I looked at Matt. "Or at least, some of you are."

He snorted at me. "Yeah, and how many bears disobeying orders did it take for them to make the switch?"

"Just one."

Sheppard wiped his mouth on his napkin. "You're sure there's a First here?"

I gestured to the scratches on my right cheek. "Met him face-to-face."

"So if we don't stand a chance against this First," he said, crossing his arms, "it's a good thing we have you around."

My rueful smile returned as the resonance grew darker. "Sure, if he were practically any other First. Except I can't kill him."

"What?" Matt thumped his fork to the table.

"I can't kill him," I repeated.

Matt threw his arms up. "So what are we supposed to do?"

"I can't let him kill her." I gestured to Lynn. "So I suggest we hightail it outta town until we can gather the support we need to take him down." If that was even possible. Lord knows I had failed the last time I tried to eliminate Zacchaeus.

"I can't condone such a course of action, Kristos," Sheppard said. "And you know that. You are talking about sacrificing an entire town to a vampire's brood."

"A brood that is virtually destroyed!" I stood and poked the top of the table with my index finger. "Zacchaeus likely only has a couple of vampires left under his control here!"

"Which he will use to rebuild his power while feeding from the innocents in this region!" Sheppard stood as well. "Innocents that we cannot let die for our cowardice!"

Power washed off him, but I was not his to command.

"*Purgatum*." Lynn's voice was quiet, her face downcast, and the melody between us took on a steely air. "What does it mean, exactly?"

"Purified," I said. "It's what the church called the last like you."

She looked up at me, the pupils of her stormy eyes were ringed in amber. "Can this First be purified? Can I do to him what I've done to the other vampires?"

I stared at her for a long moment. I wanted to lie to her, to tell her that she couldn't. It would be so much simpler if she could believe that. But she would know the lie before it even left my lips.

So, I told her the truth. "Almost certainly."

And it would tear me apart if she did.

"Then we're not going anywhere." Her voice was quiet steel. "My alpha is staying here. And I'm staying with my pack. If you want to guard me and keep me safe, if you drove all this way to do so, then you'll do it here. Because I'm not going anywhere."

I slumped back into my chair, my mind racing.

My heart pounded drumbeats of trepidation in my chest, thrumming through the music in my muscles with each beat.

Alongside it, a small syncopated rhythm ran. Her heartbeat. She was why I had come. She was what I was built to protect. She was truly alive, while Zacchaeus only played at being alive. I tried to convince myself that meant I could choose her life over his when the moment of reckoning came.

I wasn't sure I could.

TWENTY-EIGHT

THE PACK HAD all stayed at Sheppard's place that night, though Jamie and Ian ran off after breakfast to check for lost sheep downtown. With the Chateau destroyed, they wanted to get them to Blood of the Cross, their local church-run rehab center, before the feed addiction started to make them wildly desperate for a fix. Besides, they didn't know what they were looking for to try to find Zacchaeus before he made a move.

But I did.

So, I took a drive with Sheppard downtown to see the remains of the Chateau. The place didn't smell much like vampires anymore, much to the alpha's relief. But there was also no indication that Zacchaeus had even come by to see what had happened to the club.

Which left us with only one other lead.

We drove out to the gas station where I had first encountered him, but the place was cordoned off with caution tape, and a county sheriff cruiser was parked across the entrance.

So much for sniffing around there to find a trail. That would have to wait for after dark.

We'd been back at the glass house for barely a

few minutes when the doorbell rang, its clanging tones sharp in my ear.

When Sheppard opened it, the scent of vampire wafted in, along with the all-too-familiar sandalwood and cloves.

Zacchaeus.

I hadn't even noticed his dark chord humming under the bright music I felt with Lynn in the house.

Sheppard rushed the vampire without hesitation, but Zacchaeus ducked low, spinning to his right faster than my eye could follow. He dropped the phone he'd held in his left hand and lashed out as he spun, and Sheppard's right knee buckled. As he completed the spin, he came up well within Sheppard's guard, grabbing the alpha's throat as his silvery gaze locked with mine.

Power rushed through me. Likely the alpha calling his pack.

I had only managed a step or two toward the door.

Time had made my former charge—my former lover—truly formidable.

Snarls and yelps came from the dropped phone.

Sheppard growled as the rest of the pack swarmed the door. I threw my arm out to stop them, shoving as much will into the gesture as I could. I didn't have an alpha's power, but the wolves were initially created from the same stuff I was. I eyed Zacchaeus.

"Easy there, Alpha," Zacchaeus crooned without looking away from me. "We don't need three dead werewolves when we can get out of this with just one."

The chords between Lynn and I sharpened and thudded with a warrior's drumbeat. It contrasted the cool darkness of the almost tuneless harmony spilling into me from Zacchaeus.

"I could take her myself anyway," he continued. "But that would be messy. So instead, I offer you a trade. Two for the price of one."

Two? I glanced around at the assembled pack members.

He bent to pick up the dropped phone, forcing Sheppard to bend and recover with him.

Sheppard growled and Lynn took a step closer to him, pressing herself against the arm I held out, but Zacchaeus tightened his alabaster grip, his nails easily piercing the sun-kissed alpha's skin. Lynn's heart pounded hard enough in her chest I could feel it thumping against my arm as the warrior beat flowing through the chords crescendoed.

"Don't," I breathed to her. "For it may very well be the death of your alpha if you do."

Bright crimson blood trickled down the sides of Sheppard's neck. If the vampire closed his grip much tighter, it would crush the alpha's throat—and likely the bones at the back of his neck protecting the top of his spinal cord as well.

And if the wounds on my face were any indication, Sheppard's normal healing would be ineffective.

"I had been prepared for another wolf to answer the door. Or perhaps even dear Kristos here. But by sheer providence I have my hand on the alpha's throat. How deliciously delightful." Zacchaeus smiled like a cat with his prey clearly subdued. He flicked his pale eyes to Lynn and then back to mine. "Bring me the *purgatum*, and you will get your two lost pack-mates back, relatively unharmed."

He turned the phone to face the pack.

It was a video stream of two snarling wolves in cages. Human sheep held cattle prods defensively between themselves and the cages. They thrust them at the wolves anytime one threw themselves at the bars, eliciting a yelp or whine from the offending wolf.

He had Jamie and Ian. The two who had left after breakfast.

Fuck.

"You have sealed your fate, bloodsucker," Sheppard rasped.

Zacchaeus tsked. "Clearly you need time to think this through."

He didn't bother to turn off the screen or stop the stream as he tucked the phone into his coat pocket and fished out a business card, which he then slid into the back pocket of Sheppard's jeans.

"You call me when you're ready to discuss things like civil creatures, eh?" He still didn't look away from me. "And I would decide quickly, were I you. Say, before sundown today?" His voice dropped to a whisper. "What remains of my coterie will awaken then, and they always seem so peckish first thing in the evening."

He leaned close to Sheppard's ear, dragging his thumbnail an inch across the alpha's throat. I growled low in my chest, and the pack followed suit.

"Werewolves are considered a delicacy among vampire feasts. Did you know that, dear Alpha?" His tongue flicked out of his mouth and danced along the outer edge of Sheppard's ear. "And a fullblood like you? Mmmmm." His long ivory lashes fluttered closed in remembered bliss. "We flay them alive. Their screams are like music, and the fear of death rushing through their system makes the blood so very *sweet*."

"Enough," I growled.

His eyes snapped open, locking onto mine once more as he ran his tongue along his teeth, lingering on the pointed canines.

"Do give it some thought," he said as he straightened. "I'm sure I'll hear from you soon."

Releasing Sheppard, he stepped backward and

faded into smoke and shadow, the dark dissonance in my muscles fading along with him. The alpha clapped his hand to the pinpricks along his neck. As I suspected, they continued to trickle blood even with Zacchaeus gone.

Fuck.

I reached out and pulled Sheppard in from the porch, working the card from his pocket and palming it as I did.

Kaylah rushed in to check his wounds, calling for bandages.

I fished my phone from my pocket and stepped out the front door, pulling it closed behind me as I walked away from the glass house.

Two houses away, I dialed the number on the card.

It rang once before Zacchaeus picked up.

"I'm impressed!" His voice was bright and cheerful. "I did not think the alpha would come to his senses so quickly."

I continued pacing away from the house. "You know you cannot have her, Zacchaeus. The pack will not negotiate, and I cannot let them hand her to you even if they would."

"Oh lover mine," the smile in his voice was clear. "But they must. She is the end of my kind, and—in time—the end of yours and her own as well."

Fuck.

He thought himself in a fight for survival with her.

Well, he wasn't wrong.

"Do not make this choice." I looked over my shoulder to be sure I was not being followed as I continued away from the house, dropping my voice low. "Release the wolves now and I will ensure your escape."

Zacchaeus' crystalline laughter rang through the

line. "For a creature even older than I, you have always been so very shortsighted. I do not fear them,
Kristos. Not one of them has walked this Earth half
as long as you or I. They are no threat to me."

I pressed my lips into a line as the silence
stretched.

"Besides," he added. "If you were to take such
steps as you have suggested, your precious *purgatum*
may well decide to destroy you as payment for such
betrayal. Or perhaps you'd thought of that already
and welcome such death after so many years. In either case, do be sure the next call I receive is from
the alpha, will you? I'd hate to see these two wolves
die so needlessly."

The line went dead.

I stared at the phone a moment before turning
back toward the glass house.

It was going to come down to a simple choice—
kill Zacchaeus, or let him kill Lynn.

FUCK.

TWENTY-NINE

Back inside, Lynn's warrior drumbeat slammed through my veins once more, and I flexed my fingers at the sensation. Kaylah had gauze wrapped around Sheppard's neck and wrapped a splint against his right knee where he sat in the armchair in the living room as I shut the door.

Matt stormed up to me, his chest puffed up with anger. "Who the fuck was that vampire?!"

"Zacchaeus," I answered, my voice more even than I felt. "The First I mentioned."

Lynn scrunched her face up in thought. "How is he out in the daylight?"

I wiped my face and looked at her. "He's *consanguinea*."

"*Consanguinea* don't survive being turned vampire," Sheppard said.

"They do if they're turned by a First," I replied, slumping onto the couch nearest him. "Even regular humans die sometimes when a vampire tries to turn them. But not Firsts. Firsts' turnings always stick."

Matt's 'hmm' was more growl than anything as he absorbed the information.

"Well, that explains why I'm not healing." Sheppard gestured to his now wrapped knee.

"Oh?" I raised an eyebrow at him.

He shifted his weight in the chair, adjusting how his leg rested. "Injuries caused by *consanguinea* don't heal at our accelerated rate."

Injuries caused by *consanguinea*? Like the scratches on my face. I touched them, remembering the scrape of Zacchaeus' fingernails against my flesh. I finally understood why any injury from him always took so fucking long to heal. And why I didn't realize it sooner. I'd never been hurt by any *consanguinea* other than Zacchaeus.

Fuck.

A First that was likely to tear them to shreds, causing injuries they'd have to heal the slow way? This pack was doomed.

"A vampire that can walk in the day," Lynn mused. She looked at Jonathan. "Like the dream I had."

He nodded and kissed her temple as she wrapped her arms around his.

Daniel slumped onto a couch. "How'd that bloodsucker get those two anyway?"

"Well," Chastity said from where she sat at the end of the dining room table. "Since Lynn and Jonathan have commandeered the brothers' apartment for private fucking time, Jamie's been staying here and hanging out with Ian's friends when he gets the chance."

"CHASTITY!" Kaylah's voice was sharp enough that Chastity flinched.

"What, Kaylah? It's true!"

"What does all this mean for my brother?" Jonathan seethed quiet anger from where he sat on the other couch, Lynn hugging his arm.

I sighed. "He's a First, so he has the resources to get virtually anything he needs to hold werewolves hostage for as long as he wants. Further, he has the backing of powerful vampires to support him, should he decide werewolf is indeed on the menu."

"We wouldn't be the only pack gunning for him if he did." Sheppard growled.

"My point exactly."

"So he's forcing the fight now," Lynn said. "It's the only way we get Jamie and Ian back."

Sheppard nodded. "And it has to be in the daylight so he's alone."

"And it has to be today so he doesn't have the opportunity to bring in the backup of his brood," Matt added.

I turned to Sheppard. "This is a ploy to get Lynn in the same room as him. He will kill those two wolves whether you go storming in there or not. All you're going to do is hand him your entire pack on a silver platter."

Lynn released Jonathan's arm and scooted forward on the couch, to the edge of the seat. "So help us stop him."

I shook my head. "You don't understand. I *cannot* kill him. I may be strong enough, I may be motivated enough, I may be capable enough, but I cannot. He is *consanguinea*. It is in the very makeup of who I am that I cannot kill him."

"We're going in there whether you help us or not." Sheppard's voice was steely resolve as he reached for his back pocket.

I stood and handed him Zacchaeus' card as he arched an eyebrow at me. "You fuckers should've been werebears."

"What the hell do you mean by that?" Matt barked.

I spun and faced him. "The church favored wolves because you were cautious and smart. We were wanton violence. The church simply pointed us in a direction and got out of our way." I turned back to the alpha. "Look, Shep. If you had a whole pack as old and as powerful as you, you might stand a chance. But you don't. You have a pack full of pups that weren't born to this and a *purgatum* that barely understands what she is. I'm sure all of them are strong and scrappy. Hell, I can feel as much with the stability and warmth running through the pack. Lord knows they're connected to you unlike any pack I've seen you with thus far. But Zacchaeus is more than three times your age. And a First to boot. You can't just storm in there and expect to be able to take him down. You need backup. Firepower. Ordinance. I'm not enough."

"Please," Matt scoffed. "I can take down seven vamps on my own."

"Young ones like from the club downtown?" I eyed him up and down, sizing him up. "Sure."

"But really old vamps get scary powerful," Jonathan said.

I nodded. "Exactly."

"Yeah, yeah," Matt said, folding his arms across his chest as he leaned a shoulder against the wall.

Sheppard raked fingers through his sandy blond hair. "We don't have time to get the military involved. And even if I could get the kind of backup you suggest, I can't get it here before he starts killing my pack."

"I just need to get close to him," Lynn said. "Close enough to touch him. If I can, he's finished."

"That's a real big if," I told her.

"But if anyone can get me there, it's you, right?"

I furrowed my brow. "You want to just storm in there and aim straight for him?"

She nodded. "It's pretty much all we got. Hit him hard, take him down like we did with you out back yesterday. I touch him, he dusts. We break out Ian and Jamie and get out of there."

Sheppard's voice was like a father praising a child. "Not a bad plan."

Sure, if the pack was older, tougher.

As it was, we'd be lucky if he didn't kill everyone as we came in.

"The longer we debate this, the more time he has to be ready." Matt cracked his knuckles and looked at me. "Lynn's plan has a chance of working, doesn't it?"

I pressed my lips into a line and nodded begrudgingly. "Let's hope it is enough"

"We *have to* be enough." Lynn's voice held such conviction that each word thrummed its own chord into the resonance alongside her warrior drumbeat.

And in that crucial moment, for just a second, I believed her.

THIRTY

Sheppard dialed the number on the card, putting the call on speakerphone. As he had when I called him, Zacchaeus answered on the first ring.

"Ahh, the Alpha, I presume?"

"Have it your way, bloodsucker," Sheppard growled. "Give me the location of my packmates, and I shall meet you there with the *purgatum*, as requested."

"Uh huh." He raised his voice. "Oh Kristos, dear. He intends to bring the entire pack, yourself included, does he not?"

Chastity's head whipped toward me, her hazel eyes flashing with anger, her vanilla scent sharpening to prick at my nostrils.

I closed my hands into tight fists. My knuckles cracked as I remembered the promise I had made the day he was turned. A promise he had clearly not forgotten.

I would never lie to him.

But I could stay silent.

I stared at the phone.

"Kristos." Zacchaeus drew out my name. His voice was more firm, a warning in the tone. "Tell me, or I shall destroy one of the wolves for the annoyance."

Fuck.

"He does." It was more frustrated growl than words.

Lynn's eyebrows shot up, the harmony falling to a darker chord, and I looked away from the entire pack in shame.

"I thought he might." Zacchaeus was smug. "Truthfully, I had planned on it. I'll send you coordinates, then. Do not dawdle, Alpha. I'm not sure your wolves would survive it."

The line went dead.

Matt stormed up to me, shoving my shoulder. "Why did you tell him that?!"

Meeting his gaze with a growl, I stood and grabbed the front of his shirt at the shoulders, shoving him until his back hit the far wall of the living room. His resistance didn't even slow me down.

Sheppard stood, as did the rest of the pack.

Matt shoved against me, snarling like a wild thing caught, but I held firm, my fists pressed into the hollow under the ends of his collarbone.

"It doesn't matter." My nose was nearly touching his. "You will all be lucky to escape with your lives."

"We had the element of surprise!" His snarl showed his extended canines and I could not help the challenging smile that crept across my face.

"He'll kill my brother!" Jonathan's voice was desperate as he grabbed my arm and tried to pull it away from Matt. Might as well have been trying to topple a mountain.

I looked at him. "He won't. Your brother would be dead already."

Matt stopped fighting against me then. "He wanted to take them out of the fight."

"No." I shook my head, shoving him against the wall one last time before releasing him. "He wanted to instigate the fight in the first place."

Sheppard's phone dinged and he looked down at it, thumbing at the screen. "Coordinates. And a photo."

He turned the phone toward the pack. It was a dirt driveway surrounded by trees and brush.

"What the hell?" Jonathan asked.

Lynn studied the screen, her brow furrowed. "Where the hell is that?"

Sheppard turned the phone back around and thumbed at the screen some more. "The coordinates are on the far side of town. Outside the city proper, to the east. But there's nothing there, according to the maps, other than scrub and trees."

I raked a hand through my hair. "You have a better idea?"

"No." Sheppard shook his head. "I'll forward you the picture and a location you'll actually be able to navigate to. We'll take both trucks, and change there."

I nodded.

Outside, Matt and Chastity joined Sheppard in the cab of his Ram, while Daniel and Kaylah hopped up into the bed. I took my bag and jeweler's kit out of my truck, moving them into the house before coming back outside.

Lynn and Jonathan had settled themselves in the cab of my truck.

I got in the driver's seat. "I thought you would have preferred riding with Sheppard."

Jonathan grinned at me. "They're packed in like sardines in the Ram. So it was either join Kaylah and Daniel in the bed of the Ram or ride with you."

Lynn rolled a shoulder as the song between us ratcheted into a nervous chord. "We figured it'd be silly to leave these seats empty just because we only met you yesterday."

I started the truck as I pulled up the map location Sheppard had sent me. It was out on I-24, past the city proper. I started the navigation as I took one more look at the photo of the dirt driveway, committing it to memory.

Settling her back against the cab as she sat in the bed of the Ram, Kaylah pulled her blonde hair back with a tie as Sheppard backed out of his spot in front of the glass house. I followed him, the navigation chirping along, confirming our route as we drove.

Thirty minutes later, we pulled off the highway onto a farm road that led to some trees which soon matched the photo.

Damn.

If you didn't know this was where you were supposed to be, you'd never find it. And it was far enough away from whatever the vampires had going on back in the trees that you didn't smell them on the wind. No accidental visitors here, that's for certain.

"Good hiding spot for them," Jonathan said.

I pressed my lips into a line and nodded as we pulled into the trees. About a hundred yards in, the dirt road gave way to smooth pavement. And half a mile beyond that, the road brought us to a warehouse: a one-story building, low and long and squat with a metal roof like an airplane hangar. It had ten drive-up bays all in a row with the kind of roll up doors you see on the back side of mechanic shops.

We pulled alongside the building, parking on the short side to the south. We cut the engines almost in unison and Sheppard hopped out of his truck. Jonathan opened the door to mine as Sheppard looked us over.

"Lynn, your instincts are good, but you haven't been a wolf long enough to be familiar with that form. Let's keep you on two legs and let your instincts work for you." He nodded to me. "Same for you, Kristos. You have history with this vamp, so you stand a chance of keeping negotiations civil. Though I suspect we're in for a fight no matter what. The rest of you, get changed and wait here for the whistle."

Lynn nodded, and the rest of the pack started peeling off their clothes, tossing them into the bed of Sheppard's truck.

Jonathan dropped the tailgate before doing the same. "So we can hop back up easier afterward."

"Assuming any of you can still walk then," I said grimly, pulling the old strip of leather from my pocket and tying my hair back.

He opened his mouth to reply, but I turned my back to give the women what modesty I could while the change took the pack from naked bodies to their wolf forms.

THIRTY-ONE

SHEPPARD and I stepped around the corner of the building, toward the roll-up doors, Lynn following close behind us. The music between us had gained an air of trepidation, though I tried to pour confidence into the beat as we walked past the first of the warehouse doors.

Zacchaeus stepped around the far corner of the string of warehouse bays and approached us. He wore white linen pants over brown boots and a white button-down shirt. His hands were covered in pale brown gloves, their cuffs disappearing into the sleeves of his grey leather coat. It looked like a rifle was strapped to his back, but I couldn't be sure until he got closer. A gust of wind grabbed the outside edge of his coat, pulling it away from his body to reveal the gladius sheathed on the belt against his right side.

The dark resonance between him and me returned in a minor key that was a sharp contrast to Lynn's. The dissonance was disorienting. But then I focused on the chords, peeling them apart from one another in my mind until I had the melody of each *consanguinea* clearly separate from the other.

As he got closer, he pulled on a grey hooded face mask that left only his eyes exposed. He shouldered the gun strapped to his back, holding it lazily as he strolled toward us. It looked like the one Langley had shot me with downtown.

A tranquilizer gun. For Lynn.

And a mask that left only a sliver of skin uncovered.

Fuck.

I stepped in front of her, ruining his chances of a clear shot. I couldn't see his mouth, but his rueful smile touched his eyes. He'd have to bring it around and aim it if he wanted to actually shoot her with it, but I wasn't taking any chances.

"That's close enough," Sheppard said when Zacchaeus was within ten feet of us.

He stopped and nodded once. "Call the rest of them in, Alpha. We wouldn't want anyone to be late to the party."

I looked at my former lover, my heart pounding in my ears. "Still time for you to get out of this alive, Zacchaeus."

He jerked his chin at me. "I could say the same for you, Kristos. You've thrown your lot in with the enemy. But I'm perfectly willing to let all of them—and you—walk away if you simply hand her over."

He reached a hand toward Lynn. I stepped toward him, ensuring he would have to move if he wanted to even look at her.

He didn't have a heartbeat. He had not even fed to give himself the benefit of a blood boost for this fight. He knew he had this well in hand.

"We'll need proof my packmates are alive and well," Sheppard said coolly.

Zacchaeus turned his gaze to Sheppard, frustration in his eyes as he balled his outstretched hand into a fist and brought it back to his side. "Still playing this as if you actually intend to make a trade, are you, Alpha? Very well, then. Let us go through the formalities." With a shake of his head, he pulled a small remote from his pocket and pressed a button.

He still hadn't taken the tranq gun off his shoulder.

The door to the fourth bay started to roll up. The scent of arcing electricity and singed fur danced on the breeze as the door opened. There, set along the north wall about three feet back from the door, were two eight-foot by eight-foot steel cages, as tall as they were wide, with electricity humming along bars as big around as my wrist.

Zacchaeus turned his back to us as he stepped into the otherwise empty warehouse bay.

We fanned out between him and the open door as we approached the cages.

Relief washed through Lynn's song.

The cage closest to the door held a black wolf with brown highlights. His vaguely motor oil scent matched the drowsy wolf I had met the day before— Jamie. In the cage next to him was a coppery red wolf with creamy white legs and belly. That must have been Ian. His orange-and-chocolate scent was sharp with anger, but both wolves howled their appreciation at the sight of their alpha.

"I would not kill you, you know." Zacchaeus eyed Lynn as he turned back to us. "It would be a waste to lose such power. But you have not yet grown accustomed to being a wolf, and being a vampire is not terribly different, all told."

Lynn's voice was resolute. "That's not going to happen."

"We shall see," he replied. "It does not hurt, if that's the concern."

"It's not," she growled.

"Release them," Sheppard ordered.

Zacchaeus' laugh was melodious, sending a bright note through his dark melody. "I am not yours to command, Alpha. A trade has not been made. Your *purgatum* has not yet agreed to join me."

"And she won't." Sheppard gave Zacchaeus a feral smile before letting out a quick, shrill whistle.

I grabbed Lynn's wrist and yanked her behind me before Zacchaeus could get the tranq gun aimed. That he was holding it so casually was likely the only reason she didn't get taken out of the fight early.

A moment later, the pack barreled into the warehouse bay, leaping over one another as they tried to get a grip on Zacchaeus. But he was a blur of motion, and the tranq gun hit the ground before even going off. Over and over the jaws from one wolf or another snapped shut a fraction of a second too late. Almost catching his arm here, or his leg there. Sheppard was not as quick as he should have been on his blown out knee, and Zacchaeus knew it. He dodged every pounce and attack from the wolves on four legs. When Sheppard finally found an opening and stepped in, he dodged him too, baiting the alpha closer until he finally kicked into the side of Sheppard's knee, shattering the splint into the already demolished joint as blood spattered on the ground.

The wolves in the electrified cages began throwing themselves at the bars as they snarled and growled and barked their hatred for the vampire that held them.

With an amused snarl, Zacchaeus pulled the gladius free from its sheath. I stepped in then, trying to restrain him, but he was faster than I was, and slashed at the pack, who had managed to keep their injuries superficial thus far.

"I can't track him," Lynn said with a growl. "He's too fast."

She couldn't even get a hold on his coat as it flapped around him. She was just too young. The whole pack was just too young.

"Vampires are faster than wolves, pup," Zacchaeus taunted her, laughter in his voice. "Join me and this violence ends. You, too, can be this fast."

"Like hell, bloodsucker." She grabbed for him again, this time managing to grip a corner of his coat, but a slice from his gladius removed the corner from the rest of the coat and she was left with a scrap of grey leather in her hand.

"You will fail to keep her safe, Kristos." Zacchaeus' voice was a mirthfully taunting sing-song as he dodged my fist and grabbed the throat of the grey and white wolf throwing herself at him.

"You failed the church." He jammed the gladius into her side and she yelped in pain as he threw her body at Lynn, who caught her packmate and lowered her to the ground.

The wolf whined as she tried to regain her feet, but Lynn put a hand on her shoulder. "Save your strength for an opening, Kaylah," she said, her voice choked. "This is not healing like you're used to."

He had the rusty red-brown wolf in his grip next, and he dodged around Lynn's lunge at him as he brought the wolf's back down over his knee. "You certainly failed Aurelia, lover mine."

The dark timber wolf with a milky and scarred eye—Matt—snarled and slavered as he leapt at Zacchaeus, and I set a shoulder to ram him as the wolf hit. The vampire discarded the broken body to the side as he caught the airborne wolf by his open jaws, thrusting the gladius through his chest and twisting. I wanted to stop short there, for fear I'd drive Zacchaeus' whole arm through Matt's chest, but I had committed to the action.

All I could do was pivot my next foot as I planted it, redirecting my momentum as I shoved the vampire's shoulder. Zacchaeus flew backward toward the wall next to the crackling cages as he flung the body of the darker wolf toward Sheppard. The bricks behind the vampire cracked with the force of the impact, and dust fell from the shaken rafters.

He somehow still held the blood-soaked gladius. Guilt, heavy and cold, filled my system, running icy fingers down my spine.

I had hurt him.

"Zacchaeus." I stepped toward him, reaching for his free hand. "I'm sor-"

"*There's* my beast of a bear," he crooned, lifting the bottom of his hood to spit blood at my open palm. "I wondered if I would ever truly glimpse the thing that had killed Longinus in my lifetime!"

I looked at the blood spattered on my hand as he sprang to his feet.

He was not even winded from the fight.

He pulled the hood back into place as he ran at me. But the black wolf with silver dusting his shoulders and tail lunged at his feet, trying to ball up tight at the last second to topple the vampire as I set my shoulder to ram him. Zacchaeus rolled smoothly out of the way, jamming his sword down into the belly of the black wolf as he recovered his feet.

"You failed to kill me when you had the chance." He flicked the blood from his blade and kicked the black wolf toward Lynn, who was advancing on him again.

The grey and black wolf with almost raccoon-like markings tried to stalk around behind him, but as he leapt to his shoulders, Zacchaeus spun and gripped him by the throat, slamming him to the ground with the wet crunch of ribs breaking as he bashed the hilt of the sword into his face.

"JONATHAN!" Lynn's cry was hoarse with ache, the pain of watching her lover take such a severe injury sending a wash of white-hot anger through the resonance. It was strong enough that it likely spilled into Zacchaeus' chords, thanks to my own shock at the intensity.

The dark wolf in the cage howled.

"You will fail to keep these precious werewolves safe," he scoffed. "Her pack lies in shambles."

The warrior drumbeat returned as she threw herself toward him. I closed distance with him as well, though he blocked my kicks with his shins and dodged around Lynn's blows, finally kicking her toward Sheppard. He followed, kicking her again out of the way before dropping his knee into the alpha's chest. Sheppard blocked, shoving him backward. He tried to follow, but his bum leg wouldn't work like he wanted it to. I tried to get an arm around Zacchaeus' throat, but he ducked and spun out of my grasp, cartwheeling without hands on the ground as he dodged the leg Sheppard had swept out to trip him. Sheppard came up on that leg, landing a solid uppercut to Zacchaeus' jaw.

He laughed as blood soaked into his hooded mask where his mouth was. "And when I kill this *purgatum* who so brashly refuses my generosity, you will have failed her too."

He kicked Sheppard's chest then, throwing him into the wall behind him. He followed and thrust the sword low, angling it upward to jam between his lower ribs until the blade scraped into the masonry behind the alpha.

Lynn had finally recovered and scrambled close by then. She screamed in anguish as Sheppard groaned at the injury. Leaving the sword impaled there, Zacchaeus punched across the alpha's face hard enough to throw the opposite cheek into the bricks of the wall beside him. He followed with another blow the other direction, and a third, before Lynn managed to get a grip on the trailing edge of his coat and pull him far enough away from her alpha that he was forced to turn his attention to her as she placed herself between him and Sheppard.

Sheppard coughed, blood spattering from his lips. "Stop him Kristos, before he kills her. He is too strong, too fast."

I wanted to shout at him, tell him I had tried to warn him as such, but I was frozen at the sight before me. My former lover, *consanguinea,* snarled like a wild animal as he faced the *purgatum,* my renewed purpose.

THIRTY-TWO

EVEN THE WOLVES in the cages had gone still, carefully positioned away from the bars while keeping nearly frenzied focus on the fight before them.

I moved around into the vampire's field of view. "Zacchaeus—"

"I know what happened to the first *purgatum* all those centuries ago, Kristos," he said, taking a step backward from Lynn as he lifted the mask to lick the blood of her packmates from his glove. "His name was Adam, if you could believe it. How fucking conceited is that? Named after the first man." He snorted as he curled his lip into a sneer and pulled the blood-soaked mask back into place. "I heard Father Lucius himself drew the knife across his throat, though the alpha of his pack had to finish the job."

Lynn stepped closer, trying to close distance, but Zacchaeus tsked at her. He matched her step with one of his own away from her.

"Wait your turn, I'm not done." His eyes flicked to me. "I know why they killed him, lover mine. The church knew even then how dangerous a *purgatum* would eventually be. Don't you see? The world was better for their choice."

He circled over to Sheppard and pulled the gladius from his chest. The alpha growled his pain as his blood spattered to the ground.

"That's why it's best if I kill this *purgatum* of yours." He flicked the blood from the blade again as Sheppard crumpled. "I'll even do her alpha the favor of finishing the job."

Lynn growled and the warrior beat in her song grew stronger and decidedly darker.

She crept toward Zacchaeus, eyes narrowed and brow furrowed, as he pulled the gladius back for the killing blow on her alpha. He spun at the last second, right when she lunged, reaching to catch her chin in his gloved hand. I shouldered her out of his grasp before he could finish the move that would have snapped her neck.

Zacchaeus laughed at me, pointing the gladius at the *purgatum*. "You do not recognize your death even when she stands alongside you."

I stepped between him and Lynn, trying to ignore the metallic scent of blood and the singed fur of the wolves in the cages. "You know I cannot allow you to kill her, Zacchaeus."

Lynn stepped back over one of the fallen wolves as she circled around.

"You can't let me kill her. You can't kill me." He shook his head as he turned his attention to Lynn, leaving the gladius pointed at my throat. "Has he told you that he hopes you can save him from his long life? That he hopes you will take the bear from him when I am gone?"

"Enough!" I batted the gladius away, knocking it from his hand as I stepped closer.

There was a vicious glint in his silver gaze. He circled away from me again, kicking the whining rusty brown wolf out of his way with the wet crunch of broken bones and stomping on the leg of the grey and white wolf, who yelped in pain. He brought his hand up to whisper conspiratorially at Lynn. "He is only angry because I've touched on the truth."

There. He took his eye from the fallen weapon. I brought my boot down on the edge of the hilt, launching it upward so I could grip it as I lunged at him.

"No," I snarled. "He is angry you speak of matters beyond your ken!"

I thrust the blade at him, but he dodged, spinning away as Lynn tried to grab his arm. Where I was brute force, he was smooth and swift grace.

He held his hands up defensively. "You should be helping me to stop her, Kristos! What do you think the church will do with her once all the vampires are gone? You and I know well she can belong nowhere with powers such as hers!"

He reached down to grab the black and silver wolf by the scruff, throwing him my direction like a bowling ball. I dodged the wounded wolf, who left a long skid mark of blood across the floor until he thumped solidly into the brick wall, where he lay still, though I saw the rise and fall of his chest once.

Zacchaeus was toying with us. He'd kill this pack.

"Old ground, bloodsucker," Lynn said, charging him again, hands raised. "I belong with my pack."

She hoped to catch his face. She only needed to brush his skin. The warrior beat sang through her harmony, louder and stronger than before.

He stepped to the side at the very last moment, his fist flying out to connect with her gut. She doubled over as the air rushed out of her and crumpled to the ground. She sucked in a breath and groaned in pain.

Power flowed into her and I snapped my attention to Sheppard, who watched the *purgatum* with focused intensity.

The whines and whimpers of the pack quieted

and then fell silent. Even the wolves in the cages laid down.

Sheppard was funneling what he could of the pack's strength to her.

It would kill the pack. And even that might not be enough.

The pounding of the bright chords thrumming in my muscles matched her heartbeat, matched *my* heartbeat.

I had to protect her.

I looked at Zacchaeus. My former lover.

I could barely feel his dark song.

And he had no heartbeat as he reached for the back of her neck, lifting her from the ground. Her face was screwed up in pain, but she grunted her surprise through gritted teeth. She reached over her shoulder for the hand holding her, but Zacchaeus flung her across the warehouse before she could get a grip. She hit the wall with a thud, the air rushing out of her a second time as she slid down to a heap on the concrete floor. The warrior beat skipped in her melody.

The power pulsed again.

Fuck.

Sheppard really would kill all the wolves if he kept this up.

The world dulled as I pushed all consciousness of the resonance I had with Zacchaeus from my mind, tried to force it from my body, my muscles.

And as the world sharpened into focus again, I breathed in the heady wildflower scent of her, pushing the metallic scent of blood from my senses.

I *would* protect her at all costs.

Even against Zacchaeus.

I should have done so from the start.

The bright music sang a triumphant chord as the world became almost blindingly sharp. I lunged at

Zacchaeus again. His dodge seemed to happen in slow motion, and I followed it this time, driving the blade through him into the wall opposite the one he'd pinned Sheppard to. He was fast, but I was strong.

"Yes," Zacchaeus crooned, drawing out the word as more blood soaked into the mask where his mouth was. "Show me more of that beast of destruction!"

Pulling the blade from him, I quickly spun him around, binding his arms in my own as I did. Now that he faced her, I kicked his knees out from under him, sending him crashing to the ground as I thrust the gladius down into his chest cavity from his shoulder.

"Lynn," I called to her over Zacchaeus' pained cry. "Now!"

With a grunt, he pulled herself to her feet and stumbled closer. The world had become so sharp and clear around her that she almost seemed to glow. The bright music and its warrior beat buzzed along my skin as it thrummed through my muscles in time with my heartbeat.

In time with *her* heartbeat.

She squatted in front of him to look him in the eye as he stilled, but her breath was labored and she swallowed thickly as she put her hand at the crown of Zacchaeus' head and pulled the hooded mask off him.

"Do not be so naive as to think my kind will not learn quickly to keep their exposed skin covered." He sneered at her. "Your power relies on touch. And if you cannot touch us, you are no more powerful than your packmates. Quite the opposite, truly, since you are so very, *VERY* young." His voice dropped to a whisper. "You think yourself a weapon, when all you truly are is a liability."

I saw it in her gaze then. Pity. She was watching a

creature older than she could fathom recognize his death.

She looked at him for a long moment and then sighed with a shake of her head. "I wish we had met under better circumstances, cousin."

She brushed her fingers along his face until her palm rested against his cheek.

Zacchaeus' expression lit with shock as his already pale skin turned ashen.

I remembered the summers spent in the covered breezeways among the church grounds. Zacchaeus' smile and laughter as he played with the other acolytes.

She kept her hand where it was, her brow furrowed as she forced herself to watch his destruction.

I remembered the young man he became, beaming at me with pride as he excitedly told me about becoming the scribe for the church meetings, sharing his accomplishments with his faithful shadow.

As bits of his face began to crumble into dust, she squeezed her eyes shut and brushed her hand to where his chin met his neck. Except the skin there had already begun to fall away, and she winced as her fingers brushed bone.

I remembered the grown-man-turned-vampire, sneaking loving glances at me as he oversaw matters with his coterie.

The daytime walks among the village outside his manor, where he often sat with me to take the midday meal.

The nights when it was just his cool pale skin pressed against mine under the furs of our bed.

Stolen kisses in alcoves.

Foot races among the hills outside the village.

Laughter ringing in my heart like it had always belonged there.

The gladius clanged dully to the warehouse floor amid the dust and cloth of my former lover.

Lynn blew out a long breath as her eyes slowly opened and met mine. They were more golden than her usual stormy grey.

Tears rolled down my face, though I could not tell if they were tears of awe, or sadness, or closure. He had made his choice, but watching him turn to ash was like watching a piece of myself wither and die.

The heavy warrior beat ebbed from the chords in my muscles as Lynn stood with another grunt and shuffled toward Sheppard.

Something metallic among the pile of clothing and ash caught my eye.

It was a little silver box, no larger than a box of matches would be, constructed the same way. I slid it open to find a familiar wooden cross on a worn leather thong.

Ice snaked down my spine, throwing a sharply off key note into the song. In the edge of my vision, Lynn turned back to me, her expression quizzical.

It was the cross I gave Zacchaeus centuries ago. When I swore to protect him. The one I gave him again as I swore I would not lie to him. I hadn't realized he would have even held on to such a thing.

And it somehow still hummed with divine presence.

It was a mark of my oath to what I was, what I *am*. An oath I had ignored for far too long.

She hobbled back to me as I pressed the fist holding the cross to my chest. Her hand fell on my shoulder, the thrumming chords practically vibrating through her fingers.

"Kristos?" Her voice cracked on my name. In the absence of the warrior beat, the music had a melancholy chord running through it. She feared for her pack, and rightfully so.

But this could not wait.

I looked up at her from where I knelt on the concrete floor and shook the dark curls that had worked free from the strip of leather from my face. "I am so sorry, Lynn."

Placing the cross in her palm, I closed her fingers around it, hoping she could feel the thrum of its divine origin as I could. I clasped my hands around her closed fist, the leather cord dangling out of it.

"I should never have let you get hurt." I met her still-golden eyes. "Please take this as a token of my oath to you. So long as I draw breath, nothing on this Earth will ever harm you again."

The power of the oath shimmered into the melody like a clanging of steel.

It was the same oath I had made to a scrawny *consanguinea* child centuries ago.

Except she was a werewolf. A *purgatum*. And she was more than capable of handling herself.

I would not fail her.

The grey and black wolf whined from where he lay on the ground.

She looked over to him and back at me, wiping a tear from her cheek. "Just..." Her voice cracked and she took a steadying breath. "Just help me get the pack back home, okay?"

I kissed her knuckles and stood, wrapping an arm around her shoulder as I nodded. "Of course."

THIRTY-THREE

ONCE WE CUT power to the cages, it was easier to see the wolves had been dropped into them from a door at the top of each one. I climbed up there and twisted the heavy lock from each latch, throwing the heavy door to each open while Lynn retrieved clothes for the pups from Sheppard's truck, backing the Ram up to the warehouse door.

I did the same with my truck once the pups were free.

Once Jamie and Ian were changed and dressed, it was slow going to gather the hurt wolves into the beds of the trucks. Most of them were unconscious, but moving them was careful work. Sheppard coached Ian and Jamie through it as best he could through his injuries. Matt and Chastity went into the bed of the Ram, Jonathan and Daniel into the bed of my truck.

Kaylah was the grey and white wolf that was still conscious, whining weakly on the warehouse floor. Lynn wiped tears from her face as the boys lifted her to join Jonathan and Daniel.

Lynn was beat up, but Sheppard was pouring blood.

"Alright, alpha," I said, looking him over as I

pulled the strip of leather from my hair and tied it back up again. "Whose upholstery are you ruining?"

He smirked at me before coughing up another mouthful of blood. "Mine."

I pressed my lips into a line and nodded as I hooked my arm around and under his shoulder. Lynn did the same on the other side, fresh tears pouring down her face as we supported him over to the Ram. She opened the door and dug around under the passenger seat. She came up with a rolled blanket that she spread across the seat before stepping out of the way so I could get the alpha into the cab.

Ian drove the Ram back to the glass house, while Lynn and Jamie packed into the cab of my truck.

"They're gonna need to shift when we get them home," Jamie said. "Once they're awake, I mean."

I nodded. "It'll help jumpstart their healing."

Lynn looked out the back window into the bed of the truck, watching the wolves there.

Probably just the one, really. Jonathan. His hitching breath had rattled in his chest as they moved him. He was probably in the worst shape of all of them.

Jamie's voice was quiet. "Jonathan... that... it was a bad hit, wasn't it?"

Lynn gulped, the harmony between us falling dark and nearly silent as she nodded. "He'll be fine."

Jamie gulped too then, placing an arm gently on her shoulder. I placed a hand on her knee.

"Please let him be fine," she breathed.

It sounded like a prayer.

I hoped, for once, someone was listening.

But there was a hole in my chest too. An unignorable ache at the loss of Zacchaeus.

The rest of the drive back to the glass house was silent but for the road noise.

As Lynn and I helped Sheppard from the Ram, power washed over me, and a dissonant chord clanged through the song. Ian and Jamie looked at the alpha and nodded, but Lynn stumbled, nearly losing her grip on Sheppard.

"What the hell is that?" I grumbled at the alpha.

Sheppard's words were slurred and his voice was weak. "Gotta get Kaylah up. She's medic."

Lynn scrunched her face in discomfort as she took a deep, steadying breath. "It's fine, Kristos. If my strength can get her up then I'm glad to give it."

"Same," Ian said as he opened the door to the glass house.

Jamie opened the tailgate to my truck. "Exactly."

We got Sheppard into the house, setting him into the recliner and propping up his leg, which rested at an angle that set my teeth on edge.

Jamie and Ian brought the rusty brown wolf in, laying her on one of the living room couches. Then they did the same with the dark timber wolf with the scarred face, laying him on the other living room couch. Since the latter was Matt, I suspected the former was Chastity. They then brought in the grey and white wolf, taking her down the hall to one of the bedrooms before bringing the black wolf with silver highlights in to join her. Kaylah, I think. And then Daniel.

Which left Jonathan.

Lynn trailed after them as they retrieved him from my truck, taking him down the hall to the other bedroom. The song between us, while bright, was still distinctly mournful.

There was too much blood in the house. The metallic scent of it all put me on edge. I stepped outside onto the porch, the melody in me quieting some as I did.

A light mist of rain had begun to fall. I looked up

and closed my eyes, letting it drizzle onto my face for a few moments. I could not help but pray it would wash the ache away as it did the splatters of blood from the fight. Maybe it could wash away the shame that Sheppard's pack had suffered yet again for my failure.

If I had only found the strength to do what I was supposed to do the day he was turned, they wouldn't be on the edge of death.

It would have saved me centuries of torture.

The almost buzz of a small engine drew close, and I opened my eyes as a little, white, two-door sports car drove up to the house.

As the driver cut the engine, a man of average height and slightly pudgy build opened the passenger side door, throwing his legs out in a stretch before standing.

He wore charcoal grey dress pants with a white button down shirt and had a puff of curly brown and grey hair on his head. He pushed his glasses up on his nose as he looked over at me.

As the driver stood, I caught the white flash of a priest's collar under his black sport coat.

Fuck. I pressed my lips into an impassive line.

If the church was here, I suspected they had figured me out.

I started to make peace with the possibility that I may have to kill a priest to keep them from taking Lynn.

The pudgy man stepped toward me. His face was familiar, but I couldn't place it.

"Kristos?" He extended his hand to shake mine.

I took his hand and studied his face.

"Pleasure to finally meet you in person," he said. "Harold Kleinenburg."

Ah.

"The jewelry broker," I said, finally matching the

face to the email signature from him. His face was rounder, his hair more grey, but it was him.

Harold smiled and gestured toward the priest, a balding man with salt and pepper hair. "This is my associate, Father Brooks."

"Your associate." I gripped Harold's hand so hard the bones creaked. He gritted his teeth, but—to his credit—he did not yelp as I expected him to.

His expression was clearly pained as Father Brooks stepped closer. The father was taller than me by a couple of inches, with the lanky build that came with old age.

The mournful music crescendoed.

Lynn.

She couldn't open the door. If she came out here—

I closed my eyes for a moment, angling my head as I pushed my will through the resonance toward the door, willing it to stay closed.

Father Brooks tsked at me and I opened my eyes to look at him.

He was watching my grip on Harold's hand as the rain got heavier.

"Now, now," he said. "There's no need for violence. Release him at once."

Practiced authority again. Like the cop in the small town and the general at the Chateau.

Only I didn't take orders from the church anymore.

"And if I don't?" I met his wrinkled gaze.

Father Brooks sighed, ignoring the rain dripping down his face. "There's no need for the power play, Kristos of Athens. We're not here to take her from you. Now release him."

I furrowed my brow at him, but released Harold with a quiet growl.

"Go wait in the car, Harold." Father Brooks didn't even look at him.

Harold shook out his hand, flexing the fingers to try to regain feeling as he returned to the passenger seat of the car.

I folded my arms across my chest. "So if you're not here to take her, what are you here for?"

"What we're always looking for." Father Brooks crossed his arms behind his back. "Information. You're going to keep us informed on where she goes and what she's doing."

"Not a fucking chance. You only just learned I'm still kicking."

Father Brooks' expression turned patronizing as he raised an eyebrow at me. "Oh Kristos, do you really think we ever truly lost you?"

"You're bluffing," I replied. "Else you'd have taken me out long ago. Made sure Bulgaria stuck."

"Bulgaria was merely a test of your survivability." He smiled at me then. "Our file on you is a mile long —probably longer. Did you never wonder why the church was always so obvious in the towns you fled from? Why they always announced themselves so clearly? Surely you don't think the church lacks the ability to be subtle?"

I balled my hands into fists, the knuckles cracking as I kept my arms crossed.

"We simply showed up and nudged you away from things we didn't want you near." He raised his voice to be heard over the increasingly heavy rain.

He needn't have bothered. I could hear him just fine.

"That only proves you haven't figured out how to kill me yet," I scoffed.

His smile waned. "We have naught but the utmost respect for the last of Peter's creations. You are a living relic. You are as precious to us as the Crown of Thorns and the nails are. Still, you distract from the issue at hand. You will inform us-"

"Like hell I will."

The father's eyes widened as I stepped closer to him.

"You're going to leave her alone and let her do what she was born to do," I poked a finger at his bony chest. "Or you'll have me to answer to."

Father Brooks took a breath as he ran a hand over his head, the raindrops leaving thin streaks on his balding pate.

When he spoke again, his voice was steadier than his pounding heart would have suggested. "You care not for your own safety, bear, that much we know. You may be nigh upon indestructible, but her pack is not." He glanced toward the house. "You *will* inform us of her movements, or we will find somewhere else for her to belong. Perhaps her next pack will not be so accommodating of her powers, hmm?"

"God damn you."

He tsked at me again. "Do not take the Lord's name in vain, Brother Kristos."

I glared at him. "I am not your brother."

His eyebrows shot up. "Aren't you? Does the day-walking vampire yet live?"

How the hell could he know that already?

I wanted to let the bear loose, to kill him and run from here. To fight something I could tear to shreds.

Instead, I dropped my voice low, controlling the anger and using it to fuel my hold on the door. "You already know he's dead."

His expression brightened, his voice disgustingly cheerful. "Then it seems your excommunication is at its end, doesn't it?"

How does the saying go? A day late and a dollar short?

Too little too late.

Still, I had been away long enough that I could not be sure what resources the church had access to anymore. And I certainly wasn't about to put her pack in danger over this.

At least, not any more than I already had by not killing Zacchaeus centuries ago.

The pang of a guilty sour note sang through the chords and I ground my teeth.

"I tell you where she's going and what she's doing, and you'll leave her and her pack alone?"

"That's the deal, Brother Kristos." Father Brooks extended his hand toward me.

I eyed it, hesitating.

"We'll find out whether you tell us or not." He sighed. "She can only bring destruction. Better we hear it from you. Better we know something that respects the honor of the old ways is guiding her."

Bile rose in my throat. "You're hoping she rises to power like Zacchaeus did."

Father Brooks' cheerful smile turned sly. "Whether we hope for it or not, she will. The question is simply whether she will do so with her current pack by her side? Or with one of our choosing?"

When I still didn't take his hand, he rolled his eyes, exasperated.

"Every major power in the world will want influence on her. And, if left to her own devices, who's to say whose play she would back? But with you by her side?" He shrugged. "Well... better the devil you know, no?"

I furrowed my brow. "She will make her own choices."

Father Brooks nodded, his hand still extended. "You tell us what those choices are, and she keeps her pack."

With a growl, I grabbed his hand.

Something bit into my palm as he firmly met my grip.

My eyebrows shot up.

He was wearing the ring I had made for the church centuries ago, a creation of mine that dated from sometime between the fall of Longinus and the birth of Zacchaeus. It was worked from silver smelted with the relics of past *consanguinea*. It had a spike, like a gemstone, to be worn facing the palm, with a channel along the band designed to capture and hold a single droplet of blood.

This time, it was *my* blood.

I bared my teeth at him. "A blood oath."

His smile didn't falter. "The only kind we know we can hold you to, Brother Kristos."

"She will destroy anything that threatens her pack."

Father Brooks inclined his head, conceding the point. "Perhaps, but your honor has always been out-standing."

He released my hand and I pressed the pad of my middle finger to the pin prick wound.

A thin line of blood oozed out from under the band on Father Brooks' finger, though he quickly closed his hand around it, keeping his grip loose so he did not prick himself.

Had they modified my design?

"As long as the information flows," Father Brooks said, "her pack is in no danger. Now, if you'll excuse me, Harold and I have an appointment to keep."

I followed Father Brooks back to the little white sportscar and tapped lightly on the passenger window. Harold rolled it down despite the rain.

Smart man.

I glared at him as his heartbeat pounded in his chest. He swallowed audibly and I caught the hint of my reflection in his glasses.

My canines were extended.

I leaned down and smiled viciously at him as he shrank in the passenger seat. "I'm sending the piece directly to the client when it's done. You will email me an address and then I never want to hear from you again."

"Th-th-they threatened to p-pull my d-daughter's acceptance letter," he stuttered. "Sh-she just got into Harvard L-law!"

"Blackmail." I ducked my head to squint at Father Brooks, who didn't bother to look over at me.

"Y-you bring in more than my next fo-five clients combined!" Harold put his hand on mine on the window.

I looked at it and raised an eyebrow at him.

He gingerly moved his hand away. "How am I s-supposed to cover her t-tuition?"

My smile turned bitter. "That sounds like a 'you' problem, Harold. One you should have thought about before *vexing* me."

He squirmed in the chair as I straightened.

Father Brooks started the car and leaned over toward the open window. "We'll be in touch."

I glared at the both of them as Father Brooks used the driver controls to roll up Harold's window.

As the little white car pulled away, I released my hold on the door of the glass house and she flung it open.

The world sharpened and I could easily track the individual water droplets as they fell.

Lynn stared at me through the rain. "They know."

It wasn't a question, but I nodded anyway.

"They know, but they won't try to take you." I looked down at the pinprick in my palm and closed my hand into a fist. "At least for now, all they want is to know where you and the pack are going."

The already mournful melody turned darker, another clang of dissonance ringing through it, and the almost-glow she had taken on dimmed ever so slightly. Power washed out into the yard and she took a steadying breath as I hurried to her.

"I'm okay, Kristos," she insisted. "I've just not been connected like this to anything. I've never felt this kind of drain before."

"Alphas draw strength from their pack," I said as we went back inside.

Ian and Jamie sat at the dining room table, glasses of water with straws set in front of them. On the couches, Matt and Chastity were back to their usual, two-legged form. Both wore sweatpants and t-shirts that were multiple sizes too large on them, blood soaking through in patches.

"But I've never been part of a pack. It's not how the bears worked even when there were more of us. I never knew what it would feel like."

I watched her hobble to sit at the bottom of the stairs as another clang of dissonance rang through.

"But I think I get it now."

She looked up at me. "You feel that too? Like the ringing of an old church bell?"

I nodded. "How can I help?"

She shook her head. "I don't think you can."

"Not unless you know how to pour that insane bear strength of yours into the pack." Matt's voice was hoarse.

"Hmm." I blinked at him and thought for a moment.

If I was connected to Lynn through this resonance, I could feasibly have an effect on her if I could push my will into it. And if she was connected to the pack... I pressed my lips into a line.

Sheppard studied me from the recliner, his left eye puffy and black. "You do, don't you?"

I raked a hand through my hair. "Maybe. We come from different stock. If it works, it's gonna knock me out for a while."

Chastity gave a weak growl from the other couch. "It's pretty obvious we're *all* down for the count for a while, you lug."

"*Consanguinea* wounds don't heal at the normal rate." Lynn's voice was quiet, like she was reminding herself more than anything, but her hope sang through me. "Still faster than a human, but not were-wolf fast."

Rain pattered on the windows as I thought. Her might-as-well-be-mate had coughed up blood as he fell unconscious, and his lungs rattled with every breath. If I didn't help the pack, she was likely to lose him, and she hadn't even realized it yet.

So, I looked over at her and reached for her hand. She nodded once and gently placed her palm in my own.

Her hand was so small.

I swallowed thickly as I placed my other hand over the top of hers. I closed my eyes and poured what strength I could into the resonance between us, praying with all the will I had in me that it could help her pack, her family.

The shining melody grew higher pitched, until it was almost painful in my ears. For a breath of a moment, I saw twinkling golden strands intertwined in an intricate web behind my closed eyelids. I think it was her pack bonds, but they were gone as soon as I could focus on them. A serene warmth flowed through me and then funneled away from me, taking what strength I had and freely offered. My body became heavy with a familiar fatigue, and my head slumped to my chest. There was movement from across the room and warm hands cradled my shoulders, lowering me to the ground.

"We're even, old bear. *That's* three." Matt's hoarse voice sounded so distant as I fell into the hibernation that followed anytime I managed to get myself hurt badly enough.

She was safe.

Her pack would survive.

And when I woke, there would be nothing in the world that would be able to harm her ever again.

EPILOGUE

JONATHAN
COLORADO SPRINGS, NOVEMBER 2019

WHEN I OPEN MY EYES, she's there, her warmth curled against my left side on the bed. She is absolutely the most wonderful thing I've ever known in my life. And absolutely the most terrifying.

Not just because she could turn me human again if she got pissed enough at me, though I have to admit that would be pretty gut-wrenching.

No.

It's because I've never met anyone in my life that makes the rest of the world fall away the way she does. That makes every other creature walking this great Earth turn to black and white, my own brother included. I didn't know what color even was until I met her.

And *that's* absolutely terrifying.

If I lose her, and I very easily could since her abilities and bloodline put a virtual—and permanent —target on her back, the world just wouldn't matter anymore. How do you go back to black and white after such vibrant color?

As I watch her, my body finally starts to tell me about all of its injuries. And holy hell does it ever hurt. There's an aching pressure in my chest that makes breathing hard, my right shoulder feels like steel spikes have been driven through it, my jaw feels like a lead weight, and my whole head feels like it's been run over by a steamroller.

The day-walker.

I jerk as I remember the hilt of his short sword bashing into my face. And the blackness that swallowed me after.

She stirs, her weight shifting on the bed. "Jonathan?"

My heart can't take the way she chokes on my name. I try to run a hand over her arm, but I just manage to twitch my fingers a bit by the time she's in my field of view.

Her heart pounds like it wants to fly out of her chest, and her stormy eyes are red-rimmed, like she's been crying... a lot.

"Dre-" I try to call her by the name that sends her heart skipping, but my jaw won't move. And it hurts like hell.

Her soft lips brush my cheekbone as she touches gentle fingers to my lips.

"Shh." Her eyes fill with tears. "Your jaw's broken. It's healing, but-" she chokes on the words.

After a gulping breath she touches her forehead to mine and I breathe in the heady wildflower scent that is her.

"You have to rest," she whispers.

Something tiny and wet hits my cheek. A tear.

"I was so afraid I'd lost you," she whispers, her forehead still touching mine. She takes a deep breath through her nose. "I was so scared you'd never wake up."

I want to tell her it's okay. I'm okay. But my mouth won't move. And my heart can't take it. I'd move heaven and hell to keep her from hurting, but I can't even move my damn mouth.

But her fingers find mine, and they tangle into a tight fist. I squeeze and push my aching forehead against hers to get her to just look at me.

Maybe I just wanted to look at her too. Tears are welled in her eyes, and she gently brushes fingers across my brows and cheek.

I slowly nod at her.

She's right. I have to rest. But I'm here. I'm still here.

Her face collapses as the tears spill and I squeeze her fingers again.

She takes another deep breath through her nose before looking at me again, and I'm drowning in her stormy gaze.

Something I can't read crosses her expression.

She looks at the door and then back at me before raking a hand through her dark hair. She hooks a strand or two behind her ear as she sniffles and sucks on her bottom lip.

Oh shit.

Her red-rimmed eyes. The tears.

And that expression.

My stomach twists.

This is where she tells me she's in too deep with all of this. With us. With me. That she can't handle everything dialed to eleven all the time like it seems to be between us. This is where she says she needs space to decide what the hell to do about being a wolf while having this crazy ability of hers. This is where she crumbles my world to ash.

And it would make perfect sense. I wouldn't blame her for even a second.

I pray to God that I'm wrong.

She takes another gulping breath and a fresh round of tears fill her eyes.

My whole damn world hangs in the balance. Hangs on what exactly those tears mean.

"God." She wipes a line of tears from her cheek and rolls her eyes like she's annoyed they're even there. "I was so scared that you would die never knowing that I fucking love you."

She says it like she's angry, but I swear to God, my heart soars. The world blurs. And I can't even tell her.

But she's still talking, her words frantically spilling over each other like they seem to do when she gets excited about something.

"And I know we've only known each other a couple of weeks, and I know we don't know everything about each other. But I know that in every quiet breath I get, when I look at you, my soul screams 'mine,' and...."

She runs her hand through her hair again, shaking her head as she takes the deep breath she usually does when she realizes she's talking too much. I squeeze her hand hard enough that I feel her knuckles pop. She meets my grip. And then it loosens as she gently brushes the wetness from the corners of my eyes, studying my face like she's afraid of what she might find.

"And that's not something I ever want to know if it's even possible to find anywhere else. I want you. I choose you. I love you." More tears spill down her face and she roughly wipes them away.

I can't move my jaw, but I can damn well make noise. I squeeze her fingers again to get her to look at me.

"I... luh... ooh... too." I try to hold her gaze as I force the sounds out, but the world gets blurry again as my heart aches that I can't tell her the way I want to.

It's not at all how I imagined that moment going. Not at all how I thought it would be to put into words the frightening thing I realized entirely too quickly about her. I mean, I hadn't actually planned anything out, but still. I thought it'd be under the stars on a run or after one of her impossible dreams.

But she gets it.

Her lips brush mine so softly it borders on torture as her damp eyelashes flit across my cheek. I want to wrap myself around her, lose myself in her, and I curse that damn day-walking bloodsucker for my injuries. For her heartache.

But if she's here, if I'm here, then he's gone.

She did it.

She took down Mister Nuke-it-from-orbit.

And she's not nearly as beat up as I am.

She pulls away and I squeeze her fingers again, trying to get her to come back with my eyes.

And God bless her, she freaking *gets it* and does, gently pressing her lips to mine again. I manage to get my tongue to touch her lip once, the ache in my jaw worth the single glorious taste of her. Her mouth pulls into a smile as she kisses me again.

I love her more than words can say. More than I can even comprehend. More than the single word 'love' can contain.

The world stays blurry for a while as she brushes her lips against my temple, my cheekbone, my chin, my lips again.

She then resettles next to me, switching the hand holding mine as she carefully nuzzles against my neck and collarbone. Her other hand gently comes to rest above my heart. Only the ache there has been replaced by an indescribable fullness.

My beautiful, wonderful, impossible Dreamer.

Mine.

KRISTOS' STORY IN CHRONOLOGICAL ORDER

BY CHAPTER

TWENTY-FIVE
SEVEN
FOURTEEN *THROUGH* TWENTY-ONE
ELEVEN
TWO *THROUGH* FIVE
PROLOGUE
ONE
SIX
EIGHT *THROUGH* TEN
TWELVE
THIRTEEN
TWENTY-TWO *THROUGH* TWENTY-FOUR
TWENTY-SIX *THROUGH THE END*

TIMELINE

WORLD OF GRACE LYNN CARTWRIGHT

---

33 (Friday, April 3)
Jesus' crucifixion — first vampire created — Kristos is born in Athens, Greece

60
Kristos' wife and children are killed by vampires

61
Peter creates the first werebears, including Kristos

100
the vampire Vsevolod (based out of what is now Russia) starts keeping human feeders, starting a trend for vampires across the world, who no longer necessarily turn everyone they come across

170
Kristos kills the first vampire (Longinus)

316
Zacchaeus, *consanguinea*, is born to a poor family in Tolosa, Gaul

320

THE CHURCH MAKES KRISTOS THE PERSONAL
BODYGUARD OF ZACCHAEUS

325

FIRST COUNCIL OF NICAEA

335

ZACCHAEUS, *CONSANGUINEA*, BECOMES A VAMPIRE —
KRISTOS IS EXCOMMUNICATED FOR INSUBORDINATION
AND FAILURE TO DESTROY A THREAT TO HUMANITY

336

THE CHURCH CREATES THEIR FIRST WEREWOLVES —
AMONG THEM IS ADAM, THEIR FIRST *PURGATUM*

340

ADAM TURNS A PACKMATE HUMAN IN AN ARGUMENT
— CHURCH CULLS HIM, SENDS HIS PACK ON SUICIDE
MISSIONS

417

ZACCHAEUS TURNS AURELIA VAMPIRE — KRISTOS
JOINS ZACCHAEUS' COTERIE

525

ANNO DOMINI ERA CALENDAR INVENTED BASED ON
ESTIMATED BIRTH YEAR OF JESUS

570

SOGA NO KITASHIHIME, FORMER CONSORT OF THE
EMPEROR OF JAPAN AND MOTHER TO THE FIRST
EMPRESS OF JAPAN (EMPRESS SUIKO), BECOMES A
VAMPIRE FIVE YEARS AFTER HER THIRTEENTH CHILD
IS BORN

590
GREGORIAN CHANTS ESTABLISHED

638
JERUSALEM AND SYRIA CONQUERED BY MUSLIMS

642
EGYPT CONQUERED BY MUSLIMS (THEN REST OF N. AFRICA)

711
MUSLIM ARMIES ARRIVE IN SPAIN

815
THE VAMPIRE AURELIA TURNS HER FIRST — ZACCHAEUS KILLS AURELIA — CHURCH RAZES ZACCHAEUS' STRONGHOLD IN BULGARIA, TEMPORARILY LOSING TRACK OF BOTH ZACCHAEUS AND KRISTOS

816
CHURCH BEGINS TRACKING CONSANGUINEA

817
CHURCH REALIZES ZACCHAEUS MUST STILL BE ALIVE (RELATIVELY SPEAKING)

1095
CRUSADES BEGIN (ORIGINALLY TO QUELL VAMPIRE UPRISINGS)

1119
FOUNDING OF THE KNIGHTS TEMPLAR (PREDOMINANTLY WEREWOLF STRIKE TEAMS)

1271
CRUSADES LARGELY END

1312

KNIGHTS TEMPLAR OFFICIALLY DISSOLVED (RUMORS
ABOUND OF THEIR CONTINUED OPERATIONS)

1320

DANTE'S DIVINE COMEDY COMPLETED

1354

THE SHROUD OF TURIN (THE BURIAL SHROUD OF
JESUS) RESURFACES

1400

CHAUCER COMPLETES THE CANTERBURY TALES

1453

FALL OF CONSTANTINOPLE

1478

TOBIAS SHEPPARD IS BORN

1492

COLUMBUS REACHES THE AMERICAS

1495

LEONARDO DA VINCI STARTS WORK ON THE LAST
SUPPER

1508-1512

MICHELANGELO PAINTS THE SISTINE CHAPEL CEILING

1517

MARTIN LUTHER'S 95 THESES

1550

VAMPIRES ARRIVE IN THE NEW WORLD (AMERICA)
ALONG WITH THE SPANIARDS

1600

SHEPPARD COMES TO THE NEW ENGLAND COLONIES
(AMERICA)

1614

CHRISTIANITY IS BANNED FROM JAPAN (UNDER
TOKUGAWA IEYASU)

1625

BUCKHEIM SAVES SHEPPARD FROM VAMPIRES

1685

MATTHEW WILDES IS BORN IN SALEM, MA

1692

SARAH WILDES, MATT'S MOTHER, IS KILLED DURING
THE SALEM WITCH TRIALS

1703

FREDERICK DUBOIS IS BORN

1705

JOHN WILDES (MATT'S FATHER) DIES, MATT MOVES
TO VIRGINIA

1712

MATTHEW WILDES IS TURNED WEREWOLF WHILE
HUNTING DEER

1719

SHEPPARD MEETS KRISTOS, THE PACK SQUABBLES,
KRISTOS OWES THEM THREE FAVORS

1720

FREDERICK IS TURNED WEREWOLF

1765
START OF THE AMERICAN REVOLUTION

1769
SHEPPARD CALLS IN FAVOR #1, KRISTOS AND THE
PACK FIGHT BACK THE INFLUENCE OF THE ANGLICAN
CHURCH OVER THE NATURAL PACKS OF THE COLONIES
AND WILDS BEYOND

1776
DECLARATION OF INDEPENDENCE SIGNED

1783, SEPTEMBER
END OF THE REVOLUTIONARY WAR (VIA THE SIGNING
OF THE TREATY OF PARIS)

1784
FIRST KOREAN CATHOLIC BAPTIZED

1861-1865
AMERICAN CIVIL WAR

1866
KAYLAH ABERNATHY IS BORN IN SOUTHERN
LOUISIANA

1868
MEIJI RESTORATION IN JAPAN LIFTS BAN ON
CHRISTIANITY

1871
FREDERICK'S PACK IS KILLED BY VAMPIRES, FREDERICK
TURNS VAMPIRE

1883
KAYLAH IS TURNED WEREWOLF WHILE TRAVELING TO
VISIT A SICK RELATIVE

1885
THE FIRST CAR INVENTED IN GERMANY (BY KARL BENZ)

1896
FIRST AMERICAN MADE CAR SOLD IN THE US

1903
PRESIDENT ROOSEVELT QUIETLY AUTHORIZES THE US MILITARY TO BUILD A FORCE OF WEREWOLVES, UNDER THE LEADERSHIP OF THEN-COLONEL GEORGE BUCKHEIM

1914
WORLD WAR 1 STARTS IN EUROPE

1917
DANIEL CHAPMAN IS BORN

1917, SPRING
AMERICA ENTERS WW1 — THE FIRST US ARMY WEREWOLF FORCES FIGHT IN THE WAR

1917, FALL
SHEPPARD CALLS IN FAVOR #2, KRISTOS AND THE PACK DESTROY A PAIR OF VAMPIRE ELDERS TRYING TO MOVE INTO AMERICA WHILE THE HUMAN MEN ARE AWAY AT WAR

1918
ELIAS CLARK, *CONSANGUINEA*, IS BORN

1919, JUNE
TREATY OF VERSAILLES ENDS WW1

1920, JANUARY
KAYLAH JOINS SHEPPARD'S PACK

1920, AUGUST
THE 19TH AMENDMENT TO THE US CONSTITUTION
GIVES WOMEN THE RIGHT TO VOTE

1921
CHASTITY MCALLISTER IS BORN IN NEW YORK CITY

1931-1936
RED TERROR IN SPAIN (INSTIGATED BY VAMPIRE
LEADERSHIP)

1935
DANIEL CHAPMAN IS TURNED WEREWOLF

1936
ELIAS CLARK STARTS SCHOOL AT JOHNS HOPKINS
UNIVERSITY

1937
CHASTITY IS TURNED WEREWOLF — FIRST BLOOD
BANK OPENS IN CHICAGO

1939, FEBRUARY
US ARMY SCOUTS ELIAS CLARK (*CONSANGUINEA*,
JUNIOR, TOP 10% OF HIS CLASS), MARKS HIM FOR
ENTRY, PROVIDES SCHOLARSHIP FOR THE REST OF HIS
COLLEGE CAREER

1939, SEPTEMBER
WORLD WAR 2 STARTS

1940, SEPTEMBER
ELIAS CLARK, GRADUATE OF JOHNS HOPKINS
UNIVERSITY, JOINS US ARMY, CONTINUES MEDICAL
TRAINING

1942
ELIAS CLARK IS TURNED WEREWOLF VIA GENERAL
BUCKHEIM'S PROGRAM

1943
ELIAS CLARK, HEALER *CONSANGUINEA*, TRAVELS
OVERSEAS ON COVERT MISSIONS TO HELP ALLIED
FORCES

1945, SEPTEMBER
WORLD WAR 2 ENDS

1947
JONATHAN HOLT IS BORN

1952
JAMIE HOLT IS BORN

1954
LORD OF THE RINGS PUBLISHED

1969
JONATHAN AND JAMIE HOLT ARE TURNED WEREWOLF
ON A HUNTING TRIP

1991
THE INTERNET BECOMES PUBLICLY AVAILABLE —
SOVIET UNION DISSOLVED

1992
NEW YORK PASSES LAW REQUIRING ATMS TO HAVE
SURVEILLANCE CAMERAS

1997, MARCH 20TH
GRACE LYNN CARTWRIGHT, *CONSANGUINEA*, BORN IN
COLORADO SPRINGS, CO

2001, September
WORLD TRADE CENTER IN NEW YORK CITY
DESTROYED BY TERRORISTS

2003
FINISH MAPPING HUMAN GENOME — THE MILITARY STARTS DNA MAPPING WEREWOLVES

2019, November
GRACE IS TURNED WEREWOLF, BECOMES *PURGATUM* — GRACE KILLS FREDERICK — KRISTOS TAKES UP GUARDIANSHIP OF LYNN — LYNN DESTROYS ZACCHAEUS, *CONSANGUINEA* DAY-WALKING VAMPIRE — MATT TAKES FAVOR #3, HEALING THE PACK WITH KRISTOS' STRENGTH

ABOUT THE AUTHOR

Born and raised in Texas, Becca Lynn Mathis has been writing since she was a little girl, and could often be found sitting among the branches of a tree, reading a book. She even used to get in trouble in high school for writing stories after her work was done.

Today, she is a graduate of Lynn University with her B.S. in Psychology. On weekends, she plays Dungeons & Dragons (or Pathfinder) with her friends and trains with the Royal Chessmen stage combat troupe, who perform at renaissance festivals and pirate faires all across Florida. She lives in sunny South Florida with her husband, their blended family, and two goofy dogs.

Be sure to visit her website and sign up for her newsletter to keep up to date about the rest of the Trials of the Blood series!

www.beccalynnmathis.com